OVERWORLD IN FLAMES

Books by Mark Cheverton

The Gameknight999 Series
Invasion of the Overworld
Battle for the Nether
Confronting the Dragon

The Mystery of Herobrine Series: A Gameknight999 Adventure
Trouble in Zombie-town
The Jungle Temple Oracle
Last Stand on the Ocean Shore

Herobrine Reborn Series: A Gameknight999 Adventure
Saving Crafter
The Destruction of the Overworld
Gameknight999 vs. Herobrine

Herobrine's Revenge Series: A Gameknight999 Adventure
The Phantom Virus
Overworld in Flames
System Overload (Coming Soon!)

The Birth of Herobrine: A Gameknight999 Adventure
The Great Zombie Invasion (Coming Soon!)
Attack of the Shadow-Crafters (Coming Soon!)
Herobrine's War (Coming Soon!)

The Gameknight999 Box Set
The Gameknight999 vs. Herobrine Box Set (Coming Soon!)

The Algae Voices of Azule Series
Algae Voices of Azule
Finding Home
Finding the Lost

AN UNOFFICIAL NOVEL

OVERWORLD IN FLAMES

HEROBRINE'S REVENGE
BOOK TWO
<<< A GAMEKNIGHT999 ADVENTURE >>>

AN UNOFFICIAL MINECRAFTER'S ADVENTURE

MARK CHEVERTON

SKY PONY PRESS
NEW YORK

Copyright © 2016 by Mark Cheverton

Minecraft® is a registered trademark of Notch Development AB

The Minecraft game is copyright © Mojang AB

Sky Pony Press books may be purchased in bulk at special discounts
for sales promotion, corporate gifts, fund-raising, or educational
purposes. Special editions can also be created to specifications.
For details, contact the Special Sales Department, Sky Pony Press,
307 West 36th Street, 11th Floor, New York, NY 10018 or info@
skyhorsepublishing.com.

Sky Pony® is a registered trademark of Skyhorse Publishing, Inc.®, a
Delaware corporation.

Visit our website at www.skyponypress.com.

10 9 8 7 6 5 4 3 2 1

Library of Congress Cataloging-in-Publication Data is available on file.

Cover design by Owen Corrigan
Cover artwork by Thomas Frick
Technical consultant: *Gameknight999*

Print ISBN: 978-1-5107-0681-1
Ebook ISBN: 978-1-5107-0684-2

Printed in Canada

ACKNOWLEDGMENTS

I'd like to thank my family for their support through this crazy writing adventure. Without their understanding of my typing at 4:00 a.m., or writing all weekend long, or scribbling constantly in notebooks when we were out, I would likely have gone crazy. I'd also like to thank Cory Allyn, my editor, and all the great people at Skyhorse Publishing. Without their hard work and dedication, these books would never have been as successful nor reached as many kids as they have.

To all the kids I've met through Skyping with your school: thank you for all your crazy, energized support. I love reading all the stories that many of you have sent to me, and I can't wait to see more. To those I see on our Minecraft server and all the kids I meet at book signings or at schools, and all those that send me emails through my website, www.markcheverton.com, thank you for taking Gameknight999, Crafter, Hunter, Stitcher, Digger, and Herder into your lives and cherishing them as much as I do. Your excitement about my books keeps me working hard, so that I can keep writing books that hopefully you will love.

A big THANK YOU goes out to our dream team of Christine Jones, Inge Jacobs, Carol Piotrowski, Hilary Northrop, and Shari Thomas. Your help, support, understanding, and dedication have had a powerful and positive impact on us all. We are forever in your debt.

Don't judge your value by your popularity or importance; rather, judge yourself by the quality of the friends you surround yourself with.

CHAPTER 1

SCAR

Gameknight999 scanned his surroundings from atop his black-and-white spotted horse, expecting a horde of spiders or an army of skeletons to attack at any minute. But all he could hear were the *moos* and *oinks* and *clucks* of friendly animals. Tall, dark oak trees stretched up into the air; their branches spread out in all directions, forming a leafy canopy that blotted out the sky. Shafts of golden sunlight illuminated the forest floor in patches. Behind him, Gameknight's companions rode in silence as they enjoyed the moment of peaceful tranquility.

"I'd forgotten how nice it can be when we aren't battling hostile mobs," Stitcher finally said.

Gameknight turned and gazed at his friend. Stitcher, Hunter's younger sister, rode next to her sibling. Their red curls hung down around their shoulders. Each of the girls held an enchanted bow; purple waves of magic pulsed along the length of the weapons, casting an iridescent violet light on the forest around them.

"Yeah," Hunter added. "When the User-that-is-not-a-user hasn't angered the monster kings and convinced their forces to chase us all over Minecraft . . . it can be kinda nice."

She cast him a mischievous smile, which Gameknight ignored.

"It's not always my fault," he complained.

"But they do always seem focused on you," Digger added with a grin.

"Maybe it's just your sparkling personality the monsters like so much," Crafter added with a laugh.

One of the wolves walking alongside the party of mounted warriors barked in agreement. Gameknight rolled his eyes as he saw Herder bend down and pat the white, furry animal on the side.

"I feel like everyone's ganging up on me," Gameknight replied with a smile. "Everyone except for Butch."

The big NPC rode on a coal-black mare, his iron armor standing out against his animal's dark coat. In his hand, he held a shining iron sword; the purple waves of magic running up and down its length added to the glow being made by the sisters' bows.

Butch had said little since they'd left his village. Herobrine's command blocks had done a lot of damage to Butch's community, causing holes to open in the surface of Minecraft that extended all the way down to the bedrock level. All who had been caught in one of those holes had fallen to their death. Many NPCs had been killed—whole families had been destroyed in the blink of an eye—and the rage that Butch felt over this atrocity was like a blazing fire within his soul. He now spoke only in short, clipped sentences, and only when necessary.

He also had developed a short temper, and because of that, few tried to actually speak with him, except for Gameknight999. The User-that-is-not-a-user could see how the big NPC was suffering, and he refused to let him agonize alone.

"Butch, it was a good idea to ride back to Crafter's village instead of taking the minecart network," Gameknight said. "We can check on the other villages on the way and make sure they all fared well after we deactivated Herobrine's command blocks."

"Hmm," Butch grunted, but his mind was clearly elsewhere as he scanned the shadowy forest for monsters.

They continued along at a leisurely pace. Then, suddenly, the big villager veered off to the right, urging his mount to a gallop and giving off a loud battle cry as he held his sword up high. Gameknight kicked his horse into action and followed the villager. He drew his own diamond sword and steeled himself for battle.

"What is it? Spiders?" Hunter asked as she pulled up alongside him.

"I don't know," Gameknight replied as he ducked under a low tree branch.

Suddenly, they burst into a clearing, the unexpected sunlight making Gameknight squint. Butch, ten blocks ahead of him, was charging at a lone zombie. Shooting past the monster, Butch slashed at the creature, and the Knockback enchantment on his sword made the zombie fly backward. This made it easy for Butch to make another pass without having to slow down and turn. After three hits, the zombie was gone—just a trio of glowing balls of XP was left floating on the ground.

Slowing his dark horse, the villager turned and headed back to the rest of the party, a satisfied expression on his face.

"Are there any more?" Gameknight asked as he scanned the forest.

"No, just the one," Butch replied.

"You mean you charged off all this way just to attack *one* zombie?" Stitcher asked. "We could have kept going, and the zombie never would have bothered us."

"It was a monster," Butch replied. "It needed to be destroyed."

"Butch, we don't need to destroy every monster we see," Crafter said as he moved his brown-and-white pony to the big NPC's side.

"They destroyed my village, and I will have my revenge," the big NPC growled in a low voice.

"But that zombie had nothing to do with your village being attacked," Stitcher pointed out. "It was Herobrine's command blocks that hurt your community."

"Herobrine . . . monsters . . . it's all the same to me," Butch said with an angry scowl.

Gameknight glanced at the NPC and wanted to say something to help, but he couldn't find the words. Butch had been devastated by the damage Herobrine had done to his village and the people living in it, and now his desire for revenge was like a disease eating at him from within.

"Come on, we've got to get to the next village before nightfall," Digger said, purposely changing the subject. They'd learned that talking about Butch's violence yielded few positive results.

Pulling at his reins, Butch wheeled his black mare back in the direction they had been traveling—southwest—and continued the journey. Urging their horses to follow Butch, the party shifted to a gallop as they wove their way around the thick trunks of the dark oak trees.

They rode in uncomfortable silence. None of the companions knew what to say, and tension seemed to orbit around Butch like a moon trapped by gravity. Ahead, Gameknight could see the long shadows cast by the thick overhead canopy start to fade; they were reaching the end of the roofed forest.

Gameknight remembered from their last trip that a birch forest sat adjacent to this biome. The clean, white bark and the blue sky overhead would be a welcome sight. But as they left the shadowy roofed forest, everyone was shocked at what they saw.

The birch forest was burned to the ground—the entire biome had been completely destroyed.

"What is this?" Gameknight asked, confused.

No one replied; they were all too stunned to speak.

Everything was burned: the trees, the branches. Even the grass that normally coated the ground between the birch trees was charred and black. But Gameknight noticed something else about the horrific scene: countless tree trunks lay on their sides, their charred carcasses marking their deaths like silent, ashen gravestones. That was unusual. Typically, when tree trunks fell over, they disappeared completely. So why were these left behind?

Gameknight climbed off his horse and approached one of the fallen trees. Placing his hand lightly on its side, he dug his fingers into the trunk. It immediately crumbled to ash. He could see the area on the ground where the tree had once been planted, but the now-barren spot had a glassy appearance to it, as if the base of the tree had been subjected to intense heat.

Kneeling, Gameknight rubbed his hand across the burned ground. The soil was like dirty, brown glass, the result of seared blades of grass and soil melted together. Jagged shards stuck up at different angles as if trying to escape the atrocity that had befallen the block. Gameknight felt like he was on some other planet in outer space. The User-that-is-not-a-user stood and kicked at the glassy surface. The soil shattered like fragile crystal, and the ground crumbled to dust.

"What could do this to the land?" Gameknight asked as he scrutinized the surroundings. As far as the eye could see, the birch forest biome was completely destroyed. All trace of life had been erased from the surface of Minecraft.

"It must have been the monsters," Butch stated. "That is why we need to destroy them."

"We don't know that, Butch," Crafter said. "Maybe it was a lightning strike that caused this fire."

The big NPC moved to a small hill and kicked it with his iron boot. The cubes of glassy dirt fell apart, turning to dust and revealing more glassy blocks underneath.

"Are you telling me lightning did this . . . to the whole biome?" Butch asked.

Crafter did not reply. He just shook his head in shock.

"This was no ordinary fire," Digger said. "The flames were so hot they turned the soil to glass. This land will never support life again. It is a permanent scar on the face of the Overworld. If this happens again, and more land is destroyed . . . whatever is causing this, it must be stopped."

"Agreed, but we can't just go off on a killing spree, destroying every monster in sight in the hope that it might stop these tragedies," Crafter said, glancing at Butch.

The big NPC wasn't listening. He was staring across the devastated forest, his eyes burning with rage. Gameknight's gaze swept across the wasteland; his own anger was close to boiling over as well.

"We must find out who is responsible for this and make sure it doesn't happen again," Butch growled.

"I think you're right, Butch," Gameknight replied.

"They must be punished . . . they must *all* be punished," Butch said in a low voice.

Gameknight heard the anger—the unbridled, barely controlled rage—in the big NPC's voice. It made him scared, not for those responsible for the atrocity before them, but for Butch himself. *That much anger has a way of destroying everything and everyone within its reach*, he thought, *whether friend or foe.*

CHAPTER 2
CHARYBDIS

Charybdis, the king of the blazes, watched as his warriors launched their fireballs at the trees of a savannah biome. The strangely-bent acacia trees almost looked like they were leaning away from the firestorm that surged through the landscape. The flames danced across the gray-green grass as if they were alive. Tongues of fire licked up the sides of the distorted trunks, going higher and higher until the acacia trees exploded into flame, their dry leaves making excellent fuel for the ravenous inferno.

His blazes had done a fantastic job of destroying the last biome, a birch forest. They had torched every plant and tree to cinders, and then they had proceeded to melt the very soil into glass, eliminating any possibility of that land ever supporting life again. As a reward for their exemplary efforts, Charybdis had built another of his new portals, which brought the monsters to this savannah.

The sun was slowly setting on the western horizon, but Charybdis noticed, with a smile, that the sky was not blushing its customary rosy red. Instead, an ugly gray haze hung in the air like a malignant fog, staining the crimson sky with a diseased hue; it was the smoke from the raging fires. The billowing ash was rising into the air, blotting out the darkening blue sky and hiding the sun as it set its square face behind the line of mountains in the distance.

The blaze king stared at the destruction and chuckled as he took a wheezing, mechanical-sounding breath. He was a creature made almost entirely of flame and glowing sticks called blaze rods. The radiant sticks gave off a warm, golden-orange light as they revolved about his ethereal body. The blazes, the king's soldiers, were like phantoms of ash and flame, their internal fire holding the blaze rods together to form their bodies.

Charybdis shifted his gaze from the setting sun to his general down below. Slowly settling to the ground, the blaze king moved to the blaze's side.

"General, have your lieutenant deliver a full report to me after this biome is completely erased from the surface of Minecraft," the blaze king said. "You and I must return back to the Nether. There is much to discuss, and a campaign of destruction to plan."

The commander moved to his lieutenant and delivered the instructions, then turned and floated back to his king's side. Together, the two blazes drifted to a fiery orange rectangle hovering in the air. Charybdis still marveled at its appearance. The portal was like a shimmering membrane of fire that was impossibly thin, yet insanely bright. It shimmered and sparkled like the inside of a furnace, yet the edges of the portal did not flow outward as flames normally would. It appeared, somehow, captured within an invisible rectangle. The blaze king didn't really understand how it worked . . . nor did he care. All he wanted to do was destroy the Overworld and take it for himself. However it happened was inconsequential.

Charybdis gave his general a warning glance. The blaze slowed dutifully, allowing the king of the blazes to enter the portal first. As he passed through the sheet of flame, his vision wavered and undulated as it filled with orange light. Slowly, the burning scene of destruction in the savannah biome was replaced with a view of the Nether, another landscape of smoke and fire.

The blaze king moved out of the portal and looked around him. He had reappeared right where he had expected: in the large gathering chamber of his Nether fortress. Dark walls loomed high overhead, stretching upward to meet a ceiling that was barely visible in the smoke and haze. Everything was made of dark red Nether bricks, their surfaces lit by glowstones and blocks of netherrack that burned nearby. Charybdis loved the open fires, with their smoke and ash billowing into the air. It made him feel welcome and comforted. The blocks of netherrack would burn forever due to the property of its materials. Netherrack burned throughout all of the Nether. No one really knew what started the fires, but the blocks had continued to burn unquenched for as long as any monster could remember.

Concentrating on his blaze rods, Charybdis made the glowing sticks spin faster within his body, causing him to float up into the air. Slowly, the blaze king rose and moved toward the center of the chamber, soaring to the top of a central prison-like building. Windows in the sides of the enclosure were covered with iron bars, a lone redstone torch within lighting the interior. A door sat open on the side of the prison, but multiple blazes stood guard nearby, ready to throw their fireballs at anyone trying to escape.

"You said you would let us out," cried a voice from within the prison.

From his position atop the structure, Charybdis glared through an opening in the high ceiling. His eyes glowed dangerously bright as he stared down at his captives.

"You forget who you talk to! I am Charybdis, the king of the blazes, and you had better watch your tone when speaking to me, or I might get upset."

"What are you going to do?" the villager complained from the dark cell. "Put us in jail? We're already in jail. We did what you asked. We built your portals, and now we demand to be set free. If you don't, then we will . . ."

Charybdis formed a ball of fire. He launched it at the defiant villager. The white-hot sphere slammed into the NPC, lighting up the interior of the prison as it consumed the doomed villager's HP. He only had time to scream out in terror before he disappeared with a *pop*. The Nether brick wall caught fire and burned for just a moment, revealing another half-dozen prisoners within the cell. All of the survivors moved away from the smoldering wall and edged back into the shadows, hoping to avoid the blaze king's wrath.

"The thing you NPCs should learn is that it's not wise to be disrespectful of me when I have an excess of prisoners," Charybdis said as he glared down into the cell. "You are all replaceable, so it would be in your best interest to do as you are told."

"But you said if we built those portals out of Nether quartz for you, then we would be released," one of the villagers said quietly. "Sire, please have mercy."

Charybdis could see the villager lower her head and close her eyes as the other NPCs moved away from her, fearing the worst.

"Cowards . . . you are all cowards!" the blaze king wheezed in disgust. "Fortunately for all of you," he said in a louder voice, "these portals worked better than expected. I'm sure I will be in need of more of them and so will likely still be in need of your services. I command all of you to stay here as my 'guests' so that you can help me. Any objections?"

The king of the blazes formed a ball of fire between his blaze rods. The fire burned bright white and was even hotter than usual. He let it grow larger and larger and waited to see if there would be any more complaints from those in the cell. Hearing none, he let the sphere of burning death slowly fade away. The NPCs all nodded their heads in reluctant agreement, some of them openly weeping in despair.

Charybdis laughed.

Suddenly, he noticed his general at his side.

"Your fire seems to be burning hotter and hotter," the general commented. "How is this possible?"

"When that foolish Gameknight999 released Herobrine's XP in the Nether, some of his glowing balls of XP fell into the great lava ocean," Charybdis explained. "The Maker's glorious power was transferred to the lava that we all feed from, and it has given all of the creatures of the Nether more power and greater strength. It was obviously part of his plan to make the creatures of the Nether stronger, so that we could destroy the Overworld and take it for ourselves."

"Is that how you are able to light these new portals?" the general asked.

"Yes," Charybdis replied. "My hotter flame lets me light the Nether quartz ring, creating a portal that can take us to the Overworld."

"It is truly wonderful," the general said. "The Maker must have planned for this to happen when he let the villagers destroy his dragon body."

"Of course. Herobrine never would have *let* the NPCs of the Overworld actually destroy him. It was all part of his complex plan."

The general nodded his glowing head in understanding.

"My lieutenant has reported that the savannah biome is completely destroyed," the general said. "They are now returning."

The burning monster gestured to the ring of Nether quartz. Glowing creatures of flame began to flow out of the sparkling orange portal like a flood of fire and smoke. The creatures glowed bright with pride as they looked up at their king, smoke from the burning landscape billowing through the portal and filling the gathering chamber with a luscious acrid haze. Charybdis took a deep, wheezing breath and allowed the smoke to fill his senses. He could smell burnt wood and charred grass.

"Did they melt the soil into glass?" the king of the blazes asked.

The general nodded.

"Yes, Sire. They did as you commanded. That biome has been completely destroyed. Nothing will ever grow there again."

"Excellent," Charybdis said. "Soon, we will have destroyed all the biomes across this server. And when all the ground is charred to glass and the sky is filled with smoke and ash, the land will no longer support the lives of the NPCs. That is when the blazes of the Nether will flow out of our portals and take the Overworld for ourselves, as the Maker, Herobrine, promised so long ago. Soon, the villagers will be extinct and all life in the Overworld will be choked into non-existence."

The blazes that now filled the gathering chamber glowed bright with excitement.

"We will take over all of Minecraft, as the Maker intended, and then Herobrine's revenge against the User-that-is-not-a-user and his friends will be complete!"

The gathering chamber grew even brighter as many of the blazes, no longer able to contain their intense internal flames, launched fireballs up into the air. They smashed into the Nether brick roof, causing it to glow a soft orange. As Charybdis watched the display, he laughed a wheezing, hacking laugh, then threw his own white-hot fireballs into the air.

CHAPTER 3
CREEPERS

The party rode through the oak forest in silence. Gameknight was glad to see the healthy trees standing tall and majestic around him; it was comforting after what they'd all just witnessed. The ravaged forest was far behind them, but it lived on vividly in each person's mind. Gameknight was shocked at the devastation that had been done to the Overworld. Whoever or whatever destroyed that forest had done it intentionally so that it would never support life again. What kind of creature would do that?

"Maybe it was just a natural fire," Herder said as he moved his horse up next to Gameknight. His words were jolting after the long silence the party had suffered since leaving the charred forest.

"I'm not so sure . . . I feel like we're missing something," Gameknight said. "There is something else going on here that I don't understand."

"Sometimes I think you want to find a conspiracy," Hunter said. "It was just a burned-out forest, that's all. Maybe it was just a super hot fire."

"Perhaps," Crater said. "But Gameknight is right. It did seem different."

"In fact, it smelled different," Digger added. "There was a charcoal sort of smell to it. It just didn't feel right."

"Of course there was a charcoal smell to it," Hunter said as she turned around in her saddle and glanced at the stocky NPC. "There were fallen trees all over the place with their trunks burned nearly to ash. Naturally, you're going to smell something like charcoal. After all, that's how you make charcoal, by burning wood."

"But this smell was different," Digger insisted. "I've been around enough furnaces to know the smell of burning wood, and that forest wasn't the same. It had a harsh, acidic sort of scent to it, like there were potions used in the fires."

"Now *you* sound like Gameknight," Hunter said. "You're trying to create some kind of huge conspiracy here, when it was just a regular old forest fire. All the trees were burned up . . . so what? We've seen fires before. It happens all the time in Minecraft. Lots of trees get burned up."

"That's the thing," the User-that-is-not-a-user said. "Have you ever seen a tree fall over during a fire? No. They don't fall over in Minecraft. The blocks just disappear."

"Unless the ground was destroyed first," Stitcher added.

"Exactly," Crafter said, nodding his blond head.

"But how could—" Suddenly, a hissing sound came from behind Gameknight999 and interrupted him.

"Creepers!" Hunter yelled as she turned in her saddle and fired an arrow seemingly right at the User-that-is-not-a-user.

The flaming projectile streaked just to the side of him and hit one of the green mottled creatures that had snuck up behind Gameknight's horse. The User-that-is-not-a-user instantly kicked his steed into a gallop and drew his diamond sword. The others in the party also urged their horses into a gallop and shot forward.

But instead of running, Gameknight turned his horse in a tight circle and charged toward the monster. As he passed the creature, he reached out with his sword and struck at the green-and-black monster. It tried to ignite and detonate, but Gameknight did not stop to fight. Instead, he shot past, allowing the creeper to stop its ignition. Then he turned and charged again, his razor-sharp blade finding creeper flesh again and again. After three passes, the monster's HP was consumed and it disappeared with a *pop*. Almost immediately, two more creepers appeared from behind nearby trees.

Crafter veered to the right as Digger went to the left. They slashed at the mottled creatures with their weapons as they passed and kept going to avoid letting any of the creatures ignite and explode.

However, rather than following their lead, Butch charged straight at the two monsters, swinging his sword in a wide arc. Stopping his horse right in between the two creepers, he attacked the nearest, smashing it with his big iron sword. While he fought, he completely ignored the other creeper, which was slowly moving closer and getting ready to explode from behind. Some of the wolves charged forward to bite at the monsters' legs as the other animals moved to protect Herder. Hunter and Stitcher opened up with their enchanted bows. They each fired three quick shots, finishing off the approaching creeper's HP before it could ignite and hurt anyone. Butch took care of the one in front of him, then turned to see if any more were near. The area was clear.

"That was dangerous and reckless, Butch!" Hunter said. "And coming from me, that means something. The other creeper could have detonated and blown you up."

"But it didn't, did it?" Butch replied with a sneer.

"Foolish risks like that are going to get you hurt," Stitcher said. "And they might get some of us hurt as well. You need to be more careful, Butch, and watch our backs instead of just charging straight ahead."

The big NPC shrugged, turned his mount to the southwest, and continued on the trek. The other NPCs all looked at each other, exasperated.

"That was weird," Gameknight said as he scanned the forest for more of the creatures.

"You mean Butch?" Hunter asked, saying it loud enough for the big NPC to hear.

"No, not Butch . . . I mean, yeah, he shouldn't have taken that risk. But what I mean is, we haven't heard much from the creepers since the battle at the jungle temple." Gameknight kicked his horse forward, following Butch's dark mount.

"And now, all of a sudden, we find three of them . . . together?" Stitcher said. "You're right. I don't like it."

"Me, neither," Crafter added. "Did you notice how the other two were waiting for us? It was like they were working together."

"I don't like the sound of that," Digger said, his booming voice filling the forest with thunder. "Creepers that are smart can only mean trouble."

"Well, they're gone now, so they couldn't be that smart," Hunter said.

Glancing over his shoulder, Gameknight stared at the craters the creepers had left behind in the floor of the forest, deep wounds in the lush grass-covered ground. He could see the piles of gunpowder that floated at the bottom of the craters, but didn't bother to stop and collect it; they had lots of TNT and didn't need any more right now.

"We'll need to watch them," Gameknight said. "But there's something not right here. First there was the burned-out forest, and now the creepers."

"You are never satisfied unless there's some monster king chasing you," Hunter said with a smile. "Well, you'll have to just get over yourself this time. There is no creeper king trying to come after you."

"Is that true?" Gameknight asked Crafter.

"Hunter is right. A creeper king hasn't been seen as long as I've been alive. And I've been around for a long, long time," Crafter said. "The last time someone saw a creeper king was during the Great Zombie Invasion, but as the story goes, he suddenly disappeared in the middle of that struggle."

"You mean he was destroyed?" Gameknight asked.

"No, they say the creeper king just gathered his warriors and disappeared right in the middle of the conflict," Crafter explained. "If the creepers had stayed in the fight, then the NPCs might have lost that war."

"Is that why the creepers weren't punished after the war?" Stitcher said.

"What do you mean?" Gameknight asked.

"You notice how creepers don't burn in the sun?" Crafter said. "Creepers and spiders had a small part to play in the Great Zombie Invasion. As a result, at the end of the war, they were not punished. They can still live under the clear blue sky."

"But if the creeper king wasn't captured at the end of the war, is it possible he's still alive?" Gameknight asked.

"Impossible," Butch said over his shoulder, his staccato voice cutting through the air like a machine gun. "No one has seen him. It's been too long. The creeper king is dead."

"Hmm . . ." Gameknight mused.

"What?" Crafter asked.

"Well, maybe it's not that no one has seen the creeper king," Gameknight said. "Maybe it's that no one has seen him and survived to tell the tale."

"There you go with your conspiracies again," Hunter said, rolling her eyes and smiling.

The User-that-is-not-a-user returned the smile, but, inside, he was worried.

There is something going on here and I don't like it, Gameknight thought. *I don't like it at all.*

CHAPTER 4

CHOICES

Another creeper hissed as it stepped out from behind an oak tree. Gameknight was ready this time. Kicking his horse forward, he turned in his saddle and fired at the green monster with his enchanted bow. The arrow struck its shoulder, extinguishing the ignition process. The inner glow of the creeper faded, its angry eyes glaring at the User-that-is-not-a-user.

"CREEPER!" he yelled as he drew another arrow and fired.

Rather than charging straight ahead, everyone split into two groups, some going to the left while the others went to the right. The riders galloped in wide arcs, flanking any creepers that might be waiting ahead. So far, this was the third creeper attack, and both of the previous times, there had been a small group of monsters ahead, lying in wait.

As the riders moved in large, curving arcs, the wolves charged forward, barking and growling. With the creepers focused on the sound of the wolves, the NPCs were able to fall upon the monsters from behind.

Gameknight fired his bow, as did all the others—except for Butch. The big NPC charged forward, kicking his mount into a gallop as he had during the last two attacks so that he could fight the monsters face-to-face. Aiming at the nearest one, the User-that-is-not-a-user fired three quick shots into the creature, destroying it before Butch could get close.

"Butch, slow down!" Crafter shouted. "We can get them with our bows!"

But Butch ignored them and charged ahead, intent on destroying as many of the creepers as possible. Leaping off his horse, the NPC landed between a small group of the monsters. Not waiting for them to respond, Butch attacked, swinging his iron sword with reckless abandon.

Gameknight moved his horse forward as he fired his bow, closing the distance so he could shoot faster. The creeper behind Butch started to glow and hiss. The User-that-is-not-a-user aimed at the monster, but two arrows struck it before he could even draw his arrow back. Hunter and Stitcher then both fired another arrow at the monster, making it disappear with a *pop*.

That meant only one remained.

"Don't destroy that last creeper!" Gameknight shouted. "We need to question him."

But Butch was lost to rage. He swung his sword at the monster, hitting it again and again as he yelled aloud, "FOR BUILDER, AND WEAVER, AND COBBLER, AND BAKER, AND . . ." The creeper disappeared with a *pop*, leaving behind a handful of glowing XP balls and a pile of gunpowder.

Scowling down at the few remains of the monster, Butch growled and muttered something under his breath. The balls of XP started to move toward the big NPC since he was closest, as they always did, but Butch wanted nothing to do with them. He quickly stepped back, grabbed the reins of his horse, and swung up into the saddle. Turning away from the scene of the battle, he took off in their original direction, to the southwest.

"Butch, you need to fight *with* us!" Crafter yelled after him.

He didn't reply, keeping his head facing forward, away from his comrades.

Hunter growled as she put away her bow. "His recklessness is gonna get someone killed."

Stitcher nodded to her sister, then scowled at Butch's back.

They faced two more of the coordinated creeper attacks later that day, each of them unfolding the same as before: Butch charging mindlessly into the fray, ignoring the complaints of his comrades. His behavior worried Gameknight999 but not as much as the cooperation he was seeing among the creepers. The green-mottled monsters were becoming organized—and that could only mean trouble.

Eventually, the party came to the end of the leafy forest biome and moved into a plains biome, which they were grateful for. The green creatures were always difficult to see in the forest biomes because their colors blended in so well with the surroundings. With few trees, it would be easier to see monsters approaching from a distance; unfortunately, the rolling hills also had a way of hiding monsters when they were nearby. Herder had his wolves spread out, forming a protective ring around the companions;

their proud barks would announce when monsters were near. With their furry sentries, no more creepers would be able to get close to the riders.

Ahead of them, a tall hill blocked the view of the horizon as they rode through a recession. Gameknight knew there was a cold taiga biome off to the left, but the grasslands continued to stretch out in front of them and off to their right. As they climbed the hill, one of the wolves gave off an angry growl, then a sorrowful howl, as if it were watching one of its companions suffering in agony. Instantly, Gameknight drew his diamond and iron swords, ready for battle.

Glancing about, he saw his companions also preparing for combat. But before they could discuss a strategy, Butch charged forward on his black mount, galloping up the hill, eager for a fight. It seemed he always had to be the first to reach the monsters; his blade always had to draw the first of the attacker's HP. It was as if the NPC had decided that he was solely responsible for everyone's safety . . . which was ridiculous.

Urging his horse forward, Gameknight followed Butch up the hill, with Hunter right behind them. When he reached the top, Gameknight readied his swords—but there were no monsters. In fact, the party of warriors and wolves were completely alone on the plain. One of the wolves, the large pack leader, stood staring straight ahead, his fur bristling as he glared at the horizon with angry red eyes. A column of smoke was rising up into the air, likely from the village they'd been riding toward.

"What is it?" Gameknight asked.

"Fire," Butch replied.

"Is it the village?" Crafter asked when he reached the top of the rise.

"Probably," Butch replied.

A glow lit the horizon where the tendrils of smoke climbed into the air.

"You think that glow is the fire?" Stitcher asked.

"Maybe," Crafter said. "You can see smoke rising up; something is definitely going on there."

"Why would the village be on fire?" Stitcher wondered.

"I don't know, but we're going to find out," Butch said.

Suddenly, another wolf barked, and then let out an angry howl, to the left. Turning, Gameknight found another of the wolves staring into the distance, toward the cold taiga, its fur bristling and tail sticking straight out.

"What is it, girl?" Herder asked as he dismounted and knelt next to the animal.

"Look," Digger said as he pointed off to the horizon with his big iron pickaxe.

Gameknight glanced up from the wolf and saw huge columns of black smoke starting to rise. The billowing smoke was thick and climbed high into the air like dirty fingers clawing their way out of the forest. The ever-present east-to-west wind began to pull at the smoke and drag it to the west, making the smoky fingers bend and writhe with the wind, as if in agony.

"What *is* that?" Herder asked as he patted the wolf that was still growling.

"More fires," Butch said.

Gameknight stared at the big NPC and could see an angry rage behind those tiny square eyes. Butch glanced back at the village, then turned again toward the forest. More columns of smoke were rising up into the air as fires spread across the snow-covered spruces.

"We need to go see what is happening and stop those fires," Gameknight said. "They're spreading and getting worse."

"No," Butch snapped. "We go to the village and investigate the fire happening there."

"But it looks so small in comparison," the User-that-is-not-a-user said. "That forest is being devoured by fire. We have to find out what is going on. It could be same thing that destroyed the birch forest biome."

"Villagers come first," Butch snapped. He turned his mount and headed toward the village. "Everyone, follow me. Wolves . . . forward."

The furry animals barked once, then continued the trek across the grasslands, running to keep up with Butch's galloping horse.

"I guess we're going to the village," Hunter said as she took off after the big NPC, the others following, leaving Gameknight staring at the burning forest, alone.

I feel like there is something important there, Gameknight thought.

He stared at the backs of all his friends as they followed Butch toward the distant village. The User-that-is-not-a-user sighed, then pulled on his horse's reins and reluctantly followed the others. As he rode, he kept his eyes on the burning forest. The sky darkened as more fingers of smoke clawed their way into the air.

"Something is very wrong here," Gameknight said to himself, then urged his horse into a gallop as a gray haze covered the shining face of the sun, casting a gloomy pall across Minecraft.

CHAPTER 5

SCORCHED EARTH

Charybdis floated high up into the air, then settled onto the top of the tallest spruce tree in the forest. His blazes were throwing their white-hot balls of fire at the trees, severing them at their bases, and causing them to tumble to the ground. Once they were down, more blazes fired upon the fallen giants, until they were completely engulfed in flames.

With a feeling of joy in his smoldering heart, the king of the blazes formed a fireball before him and sent it streaking toward a nearby tree. The flaming ball cut the tree in half. The top part toppled to the ground with a crash, while the bottom ignited like a massive candle. Charybdis gathered more of his internal fire and attacked the fallen piece. As the glowing spheres of death hit the ground around the tree, they instantly burned away any vegetation and boiled off the thin layer of snow that covered this cold taiga biome. The ground began to radiate with a soft orange light as the soil melted into a glassy mess. Continuing his fiery attack, he liquefied more of the soil until the ground glowed as if it were in the Nether.

Charybdis smiled.

A mechanical wheezing sound filled the air behind him. Turning, the blaze king saw his sparkling reddish-orange portal grow bright as more of his warriors passed through from the Nether. They arrived into the Overworld like a victorious army, but their internal flames grew momentarily dim due to the cold temperature of the forest. Spinning their blaze rods faster, the fiery monsters increased their temperature, allowing their internal flames to grow bright and dangerous again. Some of the monsters huddled near already-burning trees for warmth.

"Get to work!" Charybdis shouted. "This biome must be destroyed as soon as possible. There is no one here to stop us, so let your fireballs rain down upon this land. Burn all the trees, then burn the ground itself."

The blazes' internal flames blossomed to a bright yellow as they gazed up at their leader. Charybdis gave them a nod and then threw a fireball at a distant tree. The tall spruce exploded in a shower of sparks that flew high into the air like the shimmering lights from fireworks, igniting the trees around it. The blazes wheezed in amazement, then sent their own balls of flame into the forest.

Clouds of smoke billowed into the air, choking out the sun that had been approaching the horizon and covering the area with a gray haze. Below, the forest was filled with acrid smoke, making it hard for him to see his warriors. The blazes now appeared as glowing specters through the dark cloud, their orange glowing bodies creating bright spheres of flickering light.

"These hotter fireballs are fantastic," one of his blaze commanders said to his king.

"They are a gift from the Maker, Herobrine," Charybdis replied.

"I love them," wheezed the commander.

"Excellent," replied the blaze king. "As my blazes feed on the infected lava in the great ocean, their fires burn brighter. Soon, with our intense fireballs, we will transform the surface of the Overworld into glass. And then we will crush the glass so that it becomes netherrack. It will be a joyous sight when all of this disgusting green is erased and replaced with a nice, rusty red."

"Yes, Your Majesty," the blaze replied. "But when will we—"

Suddenly, they were interrupted by a mechanical-sounding scream that pierced the air, followed by a metallic clanking. Something was attacking one of blazes. Instantly, Charybdis sped through the air to investigate, his blaze rods spinning in a blur. With the thick smoke, he couldn't see any attacking warriors, but the sound of the suffering blaze was like a beacon that guided him through the inferno.

A flash of orange light flared bright off to his left and then disappeared; one of his warriors was being attacked. Gathering his internal flame, the king of the blazes formed a super-hot fireball as he moved toward the dying blaze. But he was too late. All that was left was a collection of blaze rods lying on the ground.

Glancing around, he searched for the attackers . . . but saw none.

"What happened to our brother?" the blaze commander asked.

"I don't know," Charybdis replied. "Spread out and look around."

The commander moved off to the right while the blaze king moved to the left. They peered through the thick smoke, searching for the assailant, but before they got far, they heard another blaze yell out in surprise and pain. Charybdis rushed toward the sound. With his fireball glowing a harsh white, he whooshed through the smoke, ready for action. Metallic clanking sounds grew louder as he closed in on the battle.

Soon, he came upon the blaze that was under attack, and he watched as it threw its fireballs into the distance. The monster flared bright, then launched three flaming missiles in quick succession. The balls of flame streaked through the smoky air, causing it to glow orange with their passing. Suddenly, something struck back from within the cloudy shadows, hitting the blaze with enough force that it extinguished its internal flame. Clanking one last time, the blaze disappeared with a *pop*, and its blaze rods and glowing balls of XP fell to the forest floor. Furious, Charybdis fired his fireballs into the smoke, not even bothering to aim, spreading out his attack in hopes that he'd hit whatever was out there. As he moved forward, he could hear the footsteps of the attacker crunching through what little snow still remained in the forest.

Summoning another ball of fire, he floated toward the sound of the footsteps and launched a quick volley of three fireballs. One of the fireballs flared bright, indicating that it had hit something; hopefully, it was the enemy.

Moving through the charred forest, Charybdis closed in on the point of impact, another fireball ready to launch at a moment's notice. What he saw before him as the smoke cleared shocked him so completely that he lost his grip on the fireball. It fell to the ground, forming a pool of molten dirt and stone that quickly cooled into glass.

Lying on the ground a few blocks ahead of him was a collection of snowballs. That must have been what the enemy used against his blaze, but there was no armor, no food, no weapons or tools . . . just snowballs.

What kind of idiotic NPC would dare attack a blaze with no armor or weapons? Charybdis thought. *Only snowballs? That warrior was either a fool or incredibly brave.*

"Who would ever do that?" the blaze king said aloud.

"What was that, Your Majesty?" his commander asked from behind.

Charybdis ignored the question and just glared down at the deadly snowballs. These were a blaze's worst nightmare. The frozen snow could easily put out a blaze's internal flame . . . which meant the end for that fiery monster. But he could only imagine one person that would have the audacity to use snowballs on the blaze army: Gameknight999.

He'd fought the User-that-is-not-a-user in the Nether, when Herobrine had escaped that cursed Ender chest. But according to the tales from the spiders and skeletons, Gameknight999 had destroyed the Maker.

"Impossible," the blaze muttered to himself.

How could that pathetic user destroy the greatest virus ever created? He still didn't believe it.

A scream echoed through the woods as the sound of clanking metal filled the air. Another blaze was under attack from their unknown assailant. Quickly, Charybdis gestured for some of the blazes to investigate, but before they could move, the groaning sounds of the suffering monster went quiet; another of his warriors had been inexplicably destroyed.

I'll find whoever is responsible for these attacks and take my revenge, Charybdis thought. *Especially if it's Gameknight999.*

"Watch each other's backs, my blazes," the king of the blazes said. "Let us scour the surface of the Overworld and destroy everything. We will turn the landscape into a smoldering wasteland, and then the blazes of the Nether will remake the Overworld as we wish."

He gave a mechanical wheezy laugh as his internal flame grew bright with malicious glee.

CHAPTER 6

ANOTHER VICTIM

Gameknight drew his diamond sword as they approached the village. The rolling hills had hidden the structures from their view, making it difficult to see what was going on. The only things clearly visible were the thin tendrils of smoke that snaked their way high up into the darkening sky.

Hunter brought her horse up next to his, a grim look on her square face. The User-that-is-not-a-user knew from past experience that this was her battle face. All her concentration was focused on the upcoming fight, and there was nothing that would shake her mental focus.

Butch, at the head of the formation as always, charged up the steep grassy mound, then disappeared over the top. Nothing they said could get the big NPC to slow down and stay with the group. He'd been riding fast and hard, racing to be the first one to the battle regardless of the danger or the foolishness of his decision.

Seconds later, Gameknight and Hunter crested the tall hill and looked down into the village before them. It was a normal grassland village, with a collection of wooden buildings clustered around a central well. Sunflowers dotted the landscape, their bright yellow faces pointing off to the west, following the setting sun. The tall flowers were a remnant from Herobrine's command blocks and the item number replacement Gameknight had made at the last second, saving the Overworld from massive destruction. The User-that-is-not-a-user gave a sigh of relief as he thought back and remembered how close it had really been; they'd saved all the villages when they stopped Herobrine's revenge—but only at the last second.

A ring of bright sunflowers surrounded the tall cobblestone watchtower that stood near the center of the village. It loomed high over the fortified wall that encircled the community. There was no moat around the village, nor were there any tall archer towers visible. In fact, there were few defenses built into the village. *If they were to take a direct assault by the zombie king,* Gameknight thought, *this community would be in trouble.*

From behind the tall cobblestone wall, thin lines of smoke curled upward into the sky and were dragged to the west by the breeze that always flowed across the Overworld. It looked as if the smoke was coming from something near the watchtower. Sounds could be heard coming from behind the stone barricade—footsteps, many of them, were running throughout the village—but still no one came to the top of the fortifications to see who was approaching.

"Where are the sentries and warriors on the ramparts?" Hunter asked as she kicked her horse into a gallop.

"I don't know," Gameknight replied as he struggled to keep up with her.

They rode down the other side of the hill, then across a flat plain that led to the very doorstep of the village. Ahead, Gameknight could see Butch reaching down and opening one of the wooden doors that served as the village gates.

"Butch . . . wait for the rest of us!" Gameknight yelled, but the stubborn NPC charged in without any backup or assistance.

"He's gonna get killed doing that one of these days," Digger grumbled behind him.

Gameknight turned and gave Digger a shrug, then kicked his horse into a gallop and shot through the doors.

Inside the village, Gameknight999 expected chaos: a scene of destruction as the village was consumed in flames. But instead, he saw villagers calmly but quickly moving back and forth between the well and the blacksmith's house that stood near the central tower. A column of smoke rose from the half-wood, half-stone structure.

Butch charged forward, yelling at the top of his lungs, ready for battle. This startled many of the NPCs, causing them to drop their buckets in fear.

Gameknight shook his head in exasperation, then moved cautiously forward, his sword held at the ready. Off to the right, he saw a donkey shuffling about near fields of wheat and carrots, a wooden chest embedded in his hips; it was a pack mule. The User-that-is-not-a-user drew closer to the burning structure. The crackle of flames could be heard over the shouts of the NPCs. That wasn't surprising, as the blacksmith's shop always had multiple furnaces burning. But now, the

User-that-is-not-a-user could see flames licking up the thin wooden supports that held up the shop's roof. NPCs were throwing water onto the flames, trying to extinguish them.

Butch charged about, searching for monsters to attack, but there were none. As far as Gameknight could tell, this was just an accidental fire.

The User-that-is-not-a-user reached out and took a pail of water from one of the villagers, who looked up at him with curiosity but handed the bucket over. He then moved to the side of the blacksmith shop and jumped into the air, placing a cube of dirt under his feet. After rising four blocks, he stepped onto the roof, then poured the water over the burning section. The water spread across the structure and extinguished all of the flames.

Many of the villagers began to cheer, only to fall silent one-by-one as Butch stepped up and questioned them.

"Who set this fire? Was it a monster? Which one?"

The villagers stepped back slightly, confused and a little afraid; Butch still had his sword out and was wildly swinging it around in the air to emphasize his point. Gameknight placed a block of dirt on the flowing water, stopping the watery cascade, then jumped into the flow and rode it to the ground. He then moved to Butch's side and gently pushed the NPC's sword hand to the ground.

"What are you doing?" Butch snapped.

"There are no monsters here," Gameknight said. "Put your sword away."

The big NPC glanced around, suddenly realizing that there were no other weapons drawn. Reluctantly, he put his blade back into his inventory.

"If this wasn't a monster attack, then how did the fire get started?" Butch demanded to know.

The villagers all pointed to the pack mule.

"The mule got out and knocked over one of the furnaces," the village's crafter said.

"Then . . . then there is no danger here?" Butch sputtered.

The old crafter shook his head and smiled.

The big NPC kicked the ground in frustration, sending a clump of dirt flying, then turned and jumped onto his dark horse.

"The forest!" he shouted, before galloping for the village gates.

"Wait, where are you going?" Hunter asked.

"The forest is on fire! Come on!" Butch bellowed.

Hunter gave an exasperated growl, then pulled her reins around to follow him.

Gameknight ran to his horse and mounted quickly. Many of the villagers shouted questions at the riders as they left, but none answered. They all rode their horses toward the dark columns of smoke now climbing high into the sky.

"Wait for us!" Stitcher screamed ahead.

But Butch only rode faster.

Gameknight pulled up to Crafter's side. Smoke from the forest fire was now blotting out the setting sun, erasing the rosy-red sky to the west and replacing it with a sad gray haze. As the sun sank behind the horizon, the biome in the distance gave off a flickering orange glow that stretched from one end of the spruce forest to the other. It was a huge fire, but as they rode, Gameknight realized it was not getting brighter: it was grower dimmer. Clearly, it was burning itself out.

They rode hard into the night, pushing their horses to the brink of exhaustion. Finally, Gameknight put out his hand. He refused to drive the horses any harder, so he pulled back on the reins, slowing from a gallop to a trot.

The others slowed as well, except for Butch, who continued to pull ahead. But none of them cared anymore. They could feel the strain in the animals and knew they had to slow down, or they would end up killing their mounts.

"Herder, I think you should send your wolves out with Butch," Crafter said. "He'll be alone out there now, and it's getting dark; he may be in trouble."

"It serves him right," Hunter snapped.

"Yeah!" Stitcher added.

"We don't abandon our friends, no matter what," Crafter replied.

Hunter sighed and nodded her head as Herder leaned down and spoke to the alpha male. The wolf barked once, then took off running, the rest of the pack following close behind. They became ghostly specters as they shot off into the darkness, quickly fading from sight.

The party continued at a much slower pace. Eventually, they found themselves at the edge of the forest, a full moon high in the sky. The square, pale face shone a silvery light on the Overworld, giving the companions just enough light to see what was before them. They all dismounted and approached the disastrous scene. Herder placed a fence post into the ground and tied all the horses to it so they would not wander off. Gameknight cast the lanky boy a smile, then scanned the surroundings looking for Butch's horse; it was nowhere to be seen.

Gameknight stared at the devastated biome in shock. As before, many trees lay on their side, their scorched remains an ashen gray. They were nearly all composed of ash, just barely holding their original long, rectangular forms together. They reminded Gameknight of long gravestones, marking the burial place of the once-proud forest. But the most eerie thing was the silence. Not a single animal made a sound: no moos, no bleats, no clucks. It felt as if the User-that-is-not-a-user had something in his ears, blocking out the always-present sounds of the Overworld. There was nothing left alive. All the animals had either run away or perished.

As he moved into the carnage, Gameknight thought maybe his eyes were playing tricks on him. There was no color to be seen other than black and gray. Charred wood and ash covered the ground, giving the appearance that everything was in black-and-white, like on his Grandma GG's old TV. Stepping up to one of the fallen trees, the User-that-is-not-a-user could see a boot print in the side of the charcoal trunk; Butch had been here.

"He was here," Gameknight whispered. The silence made him want to be quiet for some reason. "Where do you think he went?"

"Who knows?" Digger replied.

"Who cares?" Hunter added.

Stitcher punched her sister in the arm.

"Hunter, be nice," Stitcher chided. The older sister just smiled.

"Herder, are your wolves still with him?" Crafter asked.

"Of course," the young NPC replied with pride. "They will stay and protect Butch until . . ." He didn't finish the sentence, but they all knew what he meant: until death.

"Call to them," Crafter said.

Herder put his rectangular fingers to his mouth and whistled. The shrill sound cut through the silence like a razor-sharp sword. Instantly, barking could be heard off to the left. The party ran in that direction, their hurried steps causing clouds of ash to rise up off the ground, hiding their feet and the ground from view.

The ground crunched under their boots as if it were fragile sheets of the finest crystal. Shards of reddish-brown glass flew in all directions, bouncing off their armor and adding to the dust and debris.

As Gameknight ran, he noticed the reddish hue to the shards and recognized it, but he couldn't remember where he'd seen it before. Putting aside the thought for the moment, he focused on following Stitcher as the young girl blazed a path through the devastated landscape.

Soon, they saw a group of low, white shapes materializing out of the gloom. As they neared, a taller figure began to emerge amidst the ghostly forms: it was Butch, surrounded by the wolves.

"How could this happen?" Butch said. "This forest is completely destroyed."

"We can see that," Hunter replied.

"But look at the ground," he said.

Gameknight pushed the piles of ash aside and saw that all of the ground had been fused into a dirty, reddish-brown glass. Moving farther into the devastation, he saw it had all been turned into glass . . . every last block of dirt. Whoever had done this had not only destroyed the trees and all the life within the forest, but they'd also destroyed the land itself so that it would never again support life.

Rage bubbled up from within Gameknight999. This criminal act wasn't just about burning down a few trees; it was about the complete destruction of the land, just like in the last burned forest they'd found. Questions tumbled around in his head as he tried to figure out how it was done—and *why*. The two destroyed forests were far apart . . . too far apart for an army to move from one to the other without being seen.

The User-that-is-not-a-user knelt and scratched at the ground with the tip of his sword. It crumbled to dust. Scooping up the dust into a pile, he held it before his eyes. There was a familiar look to it that he still couldn't place. Reds and dark-brown and lighter-brown and different shades of pink . . . the colors almost triggered a memory in the back of his mind, but Gameknight just couldn't quite put it all together.

Frustrated, he kicked aside the pile of dust and turned to walk away, but as he did, something gold shone through the debris and caught his attention. Was it gold ore, or maybe a zombie's golden sword? His imagination swirled with possibilities as he stooped over for a closer look.

"What is *this* doing here?" he gasped as he reached out and picked up the golden object.

"What did you say, Gameknight?" Crafter said.

The User-that-is-not-a-user did not reply. He held up the slightly warm golden rod and stared at it.

"What is that?" Herder asked as he approached, his dutiful wolves right on his heels.

"A blaze rod," Gameknight replied.

"But how would a blaze rod get here?" Stitcher asked.

"There is only one explanation," Gameknight said. "It must have been—"

"Blazes did this!" Butch interrupted. "And one of them was killed. Someone must have been here and fought back."

"There's no way one person could have fought off all the blazes that did this to the forest and survived," Digger said. "But then, where are their items? If the HP of this mysterious defender was destroyed, he or she would have dropped all their inventory, and I don't see anything on the ground other than ash and fallen trees."

"More blaze rods!" Hunter hollered. "Over here."

They all moved to the spot where she stood. At her feet were three more of the golden rods. Gameknight bent down and picked them up. They felt warm, as always; just the smallest trace of the monster's internal flame still resided within the shining rods.

"At least now we know who our enemy is," Butch said. "And we know where they are: in the Nether. It's time for a little payback."

"Hold on," Crafter said, putting up his hands to calm everyone. "We need to think this through. How did the blazes even get into the Overworld? They don't have Herobrine with them this time to make portals."

"Who cares about the 'how'?" Butch said. "We have a target! It's time to attack. We need to go to the Nether before they turn their fireballs on the villages and NPCs."

"Just wait a minute, Butch," Gameknight said. "We need to move carefully, so that we are prepared. The Nether can be a dangerous place."

"I know it's a dangerous place. I'm not stupid," Butch complained.

"No one is saying you're stupid," Crafter said.

Hunter smiled and was about to say something, but Stitcher punched her in the arm before she could speak.

"The User-that-is-not-a-user is right," Crafter added. "We need to think about what our next move should be."

"Maybe we should—" Gameknight started to say, but he was interrupted.

"You said you have a witch at your village?" Butch asked, pacing in circles, working himself up. Crafter nodded. "Then we go there and get some fire resistance potions. We'll then sneak into the Nether. The monsters won't even know we're there."

"That seems like a reasonable plan," Digger said, his eyes filled with rage as he surveyed the damage to Minecraft.

"I hate to say it, but I like it too," Herder added.

Both Hunter and Stitcher nodded.

"But what about—" Gameknight said, but was again cut off.

"Then it's decided!" Butch said. "If we ride all night and all day, we should be back to your village by tomorrow night. But I'm going to need a horse."

Herder cast the big NPC an angry glare.

"Why?" the young boy asked.

"I didn't have time to tie him up to anything," Butch answered. "And besides, he was too weak."

"That's because you rode him too hard," Herder scolded. "You need to be . . ." Herder stopped talking when Butch turned his back and headed out of the scorched forest and back to the grassy plains.

Herder glared at Butch, then turned and glanced at Gameknight999. The User-that-is-not-a-user shrugged, then stared down at the blaze rod in his hand, lost in thought. The last time they'd been in the Nether, all of them were nearly killed. Would it be any different this time? With Butch leading them, Gameknight worried that the NPC wouldn't be levelheaded enough to keep everyone safe. He had to do something to give them an edge . . . but what?

CHAPTER 7

BUTCH

Herder had not been happy to hear of the harsh treatment one of his horses had endured, and he gave Butch a strong lecture on how to properly treat the animals. But the big NPC paid little attention. He just moved his hand up and down the length of his sword while Herder talked, as if he were merely waiting for the lecture to be over. Giving up, Herder stormed away to find a new mount.

Gameknight watched curiously as Herder moved out into the open grassy plain, his wolves surrounding him. He pulled out an apple, then made a whinnying sound like a horse. Instantly, a small herd of majestic animals emerged on the horizon and came running over. They stopped in front of him, each eager to please the lanky NPC. Reaching into his inventory for more apples, Herder gave one to each of them, then patted them affectionately on the neck. They whinnied and nuzzled him with their big, wet, square noses.

Herder pulled out a saddle from his inventory. Gameknight expected the animals to run, but they all stayed still, as if being commanded to stay stationary. Reaching up, Herder put the saddle on the strongest of the horses, a large chestnut brown mare, then rode it back to his companions, letting the rest of the herd run back across the open plains.

He pulled up next to Butch. The big NPC held out his hands for the reins, but Herder held back.

"You take care of this one, *properly*, or you'll answer to me," Herder said, his face creased with a scowl. "Do you understand me?"

"Come on, kid, get down. We need to get moving," Butch replied.

"Do you understand me?" Herder said, this time, a little louder.

The big NPC stared up at the boy and saw the look of determination on the young face. He smiled and nodded his head.

"Yeah, I understand," Butch said.

Gameknight could tell Herder didn't trust the big NPC, but knew he had no choice but to surrender the horse. Herder dismounted without taking his eyes off Butch, then moved to his own brown spotted pony. The young boy jumped up onto his horse and pulled on the reins just as it started to bolt away. All of the big animals were anxious to leave the burned-out forest, but unfortunately, the path they had to take would lead them right through the scorched landscape.

"Let's go," Digger said as he kicked his big white horse into motion, heading again to the southwest. "Make a diamond formation, with Herder in the center and the wolves along our perimeter."

With practiced efficiency, they moved into position, with Gameknight999 at the head. The only one that didn't seem to know his place was Butch. He assumed he would be the tip of the diamond, so he moved his horse forward, shouldering the User-that-is-not-a-user out of the way. Gameknight gave Butch an angry glare, but the interloper hardly noticed. He just kicked his horse into a gallop, the rest of the group following behind.

"I guess Butch will lead for a while," Stitcher said, trying to defuse the tension.

Hunter laughed and slapped Gameknight on the back as she rode past, leaving him to take up the rear position in the diamond.

They rode in uneasy silence through the burned-out forest, all of the companions surveying the devastated landscape in disbelief. Everything was destroyed in the cold taiga biome. Not a single animal nor plant was seen. The blazes had completely eradicated every living thing from the area, leaving not even the smallest blade of grass alive; they had been incredibly thorough.

As they rode, Gameknight watched Herder. He knew the cold taiga biomes were one of the places wolves spawned naturally, but as they traversed the wasteland, they didn't see any of the white furry animals appear. Herder gave off a shrill, high-pitched whistle now and then to call out to any animals that might be lurking around in the area, but none materialized out of the hazy darkness.

It was as if this section of Minecraft was completely dead.

The lanky boy slumped in his saddle when he realized none would come to his call.

"Don't give up, Herder," Gameknight said from behind. "That's not the way we do things. We keep trying, and we refuse to quit. So keep searching for your wolves. They'll come soon."

"This land is dead," Butch said from over his shoulder. "Hoping for something that will never come is pointless. The only thing you can count on is what you can do yourself."

"That's not a very optimistic attitude," Crafter said.

"It's just the truth," Butch replied. "You don't necessarily have to like the truth, but it's still the way it is."

"I don't agree," Gameknight said. "Hope is a powerful thing. We've seen villagers stand up against unbelievable odds and battle overwhelming foes because they had hope that they could win the day."

"And did they *win* the day?" Butch asked. "Or were they killed?"

"Some lost their lives, but many survived," Crafter said.

"But some died. Like I was saying; those people had hope, and they were still destroyed," Butch said confidently, as if he were reciting some kind of universal truth. "You can only count on what you see in front of you. Miracles are for fools."

"You're wrong," Gameknight said sheepishly. "If there is life, then there is hope." But no one seemed to hear him.

"Butch, what happened to make you such a bundle of joy?" Hunter asked. "You've been pessimistic, angry, and generally not so much fun to be around since we met you."

"You mean back when I saved all you in the Bryce canyon?" Butch replied, glaring over his shoulder at the redhead.

"That's right," Hunter replied. "I would have been really happy that I'd saved some peoples' lives, but based on your reaction, it seemed like it was just another day for you."

Butch growled as his anger grew.

"What my incredibly insensitive sister is trying to say," Stitcher interjected, "is that we were all grateful to you and your warriors for saving us back then. But why do we never see you happy? Even when we defeated Herobrine's command blocks, you didn't seem pleased. What happened to make you so angry?"

"You mean besides Herobrine putting holes in my village and destroying men, women, and children?" Butch asked.

"Yep," Hunter said quickly before Stitcher could speak. "What's the deal?"

"You want to know *the deal*?" Butch snapped. "I'll tell you the deal. Our village always had to deal with monsters on a daily basis. There was a skeleton town nearby, and a zombie town, and a spider's nest as well. The monsters would attack every night, and our army would ride out and meet them, destroying the threat before they ever reached our doors.

"During the war with the king of the Endermen, we heard about villagers putting up walls around their villages. Our crafter talked about all of us pitching in to mine stone so we could have a massive wall, but I didn't agree. Having our warriors digging up stone was a waste of their abilities. So far, no monster had ever made it to our doorstep. Our army was able to go out and strike hard and fast, destroying them before they could ever get close.

"So I convinced everyone to keep things as-is, and let the army protect the village . . . but I was wrong.

"The three monster villages decided to start working together and lure us into a trap. A group of skeletons drew the warriors out of the village. They were seen on the plain, far out near the steep drop. We knew that skeletons are relatively slow, so we rode out after them, ready to cut them down before they had a chance to escape. But they must have been spider jockies, because when we got out there, they were gone. While the army looked for the monsters, another army of spiders, skeletons, and zombies snuck up to the village from behind."

Butch paused for a moment to scan the desolate surroundings, looking for threats. Or maybe he just needed to collect himself—Gameknight could see the incredible tension in the big NPC's body. It was as if Butch was preparing to be tortured and was summoning all of his courage for this ordeal.

"They attacked the village. The spiders snuck up on top of the homes, waiting for people to come out and fight, while the skeletons and zombies spread out through the village.

"My little brother, Harvester—though he liked to be called Cutter—stayed back in the village when the army left. He wanted to be in the army, but Cutter was like Herder; he was small and thin and not very strong. We needed big NPCs that were brave and daring to be in the army. It would have been too dangerous for Cutter. If he froze up or ran away in the heat of battle, then he might get hurt, or get those around him hurt. In the army, everyone watched out for everyone else, and there wasn't room for someone who might run. So I told Cutter he couldn't join until he got a lot bigger."

"Size is not a measure of one's courage," Stitcher pointed out. "Do you doubt my bravery in battle?"

"Of course not . . . I was a fool back then," Butch said.

"You can say that again," Hunter added under her breath.

Butch cast her an annoyed glance, then continued.

"So when the army went out after the skeletons, Cutter stayed back in the village, just like always. But this time, it was *not* like always. This time, the monsters were working together. The skeletons that we saw out on the plain were a ruse to lure us away so that the rest of the monsters could attack the village.

"When the spider jockies out on the plains saw us, they scuttled behind the rolling hills and took shelter in some caves. We combed the landscape for them, but we never found them. By the time we made it back to the village, it was almost over."

He paused to take a breath. The ash being kicked up by the horses choked him up for a moment . . . *or maybe it was the awful memory,* Gameknight thought as he watched.

"The villagers that survived the attack told me all about it when I returned. They said the monsters came in from the back of the village by wading quietly through the river that ran along the backside of the community. I had thought the river would be enough to protect our rear; that was only one of the many things I was wrong about that day."

Butch stared up at the moon that was high overhead. Gameknight thought the big NPC seemed lost in the memory, a sad smile slowly creeping across his square face. He chuckled softly.

"I can still remember Cutter testing how many blocks of wheat he could cut with a single swing. He'd practice and train so that he'd get stronger and stronger. He wanted to be the best harvester in the village. No one could best him at it—he was truly the harvesting master. I remember one time when he tried to do four blocks in one swipe with his hoe. He wound up and swung with all his might, but he swung too hard. His feet slipped, causing him to fall and hit the ground. Putting out his hands to catch his fall, he let go of his hoe. It went shooting across the farm and stuck in the side of Baker's house. The tip of the hoe sank so deep into the wall that nobody could pull it out. It stayed there for months until someone cut it down with an axe." He chuckled to himself again. "We used to ask him where he put his hoe after that . . . we'd all laugh, especially Cutter. He was one of the best of us."

"What happened to him?" Crafter asked.

"When the monsters came, they attacked the village. Skeletons shot . . ." he paused for a moment as the painful memories played through his mind. "Skeletons shot in through any open window they could find, attacking men, women, and children without remorse. The spiders climbed on top of the roofs, waiting for unsuspecting NPCs to leave the safety of their homes.

"They told me the zombies started pounding on the doors of the houses, trying to break in and infect those inside. We lost Weaver and Painter that way." He sighed and shook his head, as if reliving the event. "The blacksmith said he heard the sound of the zombies, then saw Cutter running out of our home wearing the leather armor I'd given him long ago, swinging an old iron sword. My brother charged straight into the zombies and slashed at them with all his might. The green monsters probably figured he was a child, due to him being so small and skinny. Blacky said none of the monsters even noticed him . . . that was, until he destroyed his second zombie. Then the monsters took him very seriously.

"They say the skeletons started firing at him first. Two arrows hit him before he even slowed down. The other villagers saw this, and charged out to help him. That was when the spiders came down off the roofs. They attacked the villagers and destroyed a dozen of my friends before anyone realized what was happening."

Butch reached up and wiped a tear from his eye.

"My brother ran to help Blacky. A massive spider was trying to jump on top of him. Cutter leapt on top of the monster and started hitting it with the sword. Blacky said he held on like he was riding a wild stallion. My brother eventually destroyed the spider all by himself." Gameknight could tell that Butch was incredibly proud of his brother for what he'd done. Then the NPC grew quiet, and his voice became a whisper.

"The skeletons saw this and started firing on Cutter again. Blacky and some of the others charged at the skeletons, but they couldn't get to the bony monsters until it was too late. Arrows hit my brother from all sides, destroying his leather armor, then taking his HP down to zero.

"That was when I returned with the army to take care of the rest of the monsters. We lost twenty-three friends and family on that day . . . all because of me.

In my arrogance, I thought my mighty army could protect the village better than a huge wall could. I was wrong. And the price of my mistake was the life of . . ." he paused as square tears tumbled down his cheeks, "was the life of my little brother and twenty-two other NPCs. I swore that day that I would protect my village and make amends for my failure. And as long as I draw breath, I will protect my village and *all* villagers in Minecraft."

"Butch, you can't be responsible for things you didn't know were going to happen," Crafter said.

Butch remained silent.

"Crafter is right," Digger added. "We can only do so much. You can't support the weight of the whole world on your shoulders. It's impossible."

"You don't get it!" Butch snapped. "Cutter was my responsibility. Zombies destroyed our parents when we were young, and it was my job to keep my brother safe. I failed. If I had only agreed to take him with us in the army, he'd be alive today."

"But how many others would be dead?" Stitcher said. "It sounds like Cutter was actually incredibly brave and saved a whole lot of people. Without him being in the village, more villagers would have been destroyed. I think Cutter was a hero."

Butch sighed, then turned and glared over his shoulder. "Don't you see? I couldn't see past his puny size to recognize his incredible courage and strength. It took his death for me to realize who he really was. I failed him, and many others, in our village. That won't happen again as long as I live. I will stop *any* monster that threatens *any* village, and these blazes are doing exactly that."

He turned forward, and they all could tell that the discussion was over.

Gameknight could see there was much strength and courage in Butch, but also much anger and regret. These emotions were going to pull the big NPC apart eventually. Gameknight wanted to help, somehow, but he didn't know what to do. He could remember seeing that same thirst for revenge in Hunter, after her own family had been killed by Malacoda and the monsters of the Nether. It had almost destroyed her. Gameknight hoped it would not destroy the big NPC, for he could feel, somehow, that Butch was one of the critical pieces to the puzzle that sat before them. If Butch managed to get himself killed before they solved this mystery, then they would all be in a lot of trouble.

CHAPTER 8

THE CREEPER KING

The newborn creeper tested her tiny little feet as she scurried around the many black-spotted green eggs that lined the floor of the hatching chamber. Light from a stream of lava lit the room, illuminating the space just enough so the creepling could see where she was going.

One of the older creepers—they were called tenders—stood near the entrance to the chamber, waiting for the creepling. It was the tender's job to take the newborns down to feed on a rich vein of coal, so they could begin to generate more gunpowder and become more powerful.

The creepling moved into the cluster of other newborns. They all appeared identical, their bodies a deep, rich green with pale white spots on their skin. As they matured and their explosive power grew, their spots would fill with black. Until their spots were solid black, the little creatures would stay in the creeper hive, feeding on coal and staying out of the way.

"Come," the tender said, his aged body glowing ever so slightly, then dimming again.

He turned and led the group of creeplings through twisting tunnels that burrowed their way deep into the flesh of Minecraft. The passage intersected other tunnels as it spiraled downward. The tender took a left turn, then a right, then went straight, following a zigzagging path until he reached a large, dark chamber.

All around them, the walls were lined with coal ore. The black-spotted blocks merged with the darkness, making the wall difficult to see. But the creeplings didn't need to see . . . they could sense the presence of the coal, and they were hungry. Without being told, the tiny creepers moved into the room and settled against the perimeter of the cavern. With sharp black teeth hidden inside their dark mouths, they began to carve away at the coal ore, separating the coal from the stone as they fed.

Oxus, the king of the creepers, stood back in the shadows and watched. Sheets of blue electricity danced about his skin as jagged lines of bright red sparks wrapped around his green body. The light from these powers, given to him by the Maker, Herobrine, cast a dim purple glow into the dark chamber, allowing him to watch the newborns. He always liked this moment, when the young creeplings experienced their first taste of coal. As he watched, he could hear their blunt teeth scraping against the hard stone, scratching away at the ore. The screeching sound was like beautiful music to the creeper king.

"Soon your young spots will blacken and you will be ready for the surface," Oxus said, his voice echoing off the walls of the dark chamber. "Until then, feed on the coal and grow strong, so that you may serve the hive."

The creeplings did not look up at their king; they just continued to gnaw away at the dark walls, slowly chiseling into the coal ore, gradually enlarging the chamber with each new generation.

Oxus made a strange smile that went unnoticed in the darkness. With a perpetually-downturned mouth, a smile on a creeper actually looked more like a pained grimace. He turned away from the feeding ground and scurried through the twisting passages of the hive. Moving along the halls he'd used for a hundred years, the creeper king followed the well-memorized path until he found himself at the entrance of the gathering chamber. Within the room, he could see all of his advisors arguing with each other, some of them hissing and glowing bright with agitation. As he entered, the hall grew uncomfortably quiet.

"My advisors still argue?" Oxus said.

"There are many questions," one of the creepers said, a hissing sound accompanying his speech.

Creepers can only speak by initiating their ignition process, which has the effect of keeping all discussions short; sometimes, in a heated argument, a creeper would talk so long they would explode. That usually meant the other creeper won the argument . . . as long as they weren't too close. Only the king of the creepers, Oxus, could speak without igniting; that was a gift from Herobrine at the time of his making.

"Tell me, what are your concerns?" the creeper king asked.

"The Maker is gone," one of them hissed.

"That is correct," Oxus replied. "We all felt his presence leaving Minecraft. We are free from his tyranny and no longer need to hide within the passages of the hive."

"Monsters are still fighting the NPCs," hissed another.

"Our scouts have confirmed this," Oxus said. "The skeletons and spiders were waging some kind of war, but it has stopped. The NPCs stopped the monsters from their campaign of destruction. Likely, the User-that-is-not-a-user had a hand in that."

Many of the creepers began to hiss and glow bright at the sound of Gameknight999's name. The User-that-is-not-a-user was the enemy of all monsters in Minecraft, and the creepers knew this just as well as any other.

"The User-that-is-not-a-user still hunts the monsters of the Overworld," one of Oxus's generals said.

The creeper king turned to look at the general. Blue sparkling light surrounded the creature, making the other monsters afraid to draw too close to him. He was a charged creeper, one of the few that Oxus had sent out into a lightning storm to be transformed. Now, his explosive power was much greater than the other creepers, drawing respect and fear from the masses.

"Yes, I have heard the reports from our scouts," the king of the creepers said. "We will continue to watch for him throughout the land."

"More rogue creepers were seen," hissed one of the lieutenants.

"Yes, I know," Oxus replied. "It is unfortunate that many do not wish to stay hidden with us in the creeper hive. Small numbers of rogue creepers continue to escape and prowl about the landscape, searching for users or NPCs to destroy. I know

Herobrine used many of our brothers and sisters in his war to dominate Minecraft, but now that he is gone, the rogue creepers have nothing to do. They will cause trouble, and need to be brought back into the fold of the hive."

He turned back to his sparkling general. "Send out small parties to bring them back here, into our community. We need to be strong, so that we can be ready to face the NPC threat when it is time."

Groups of creepers scurried out of the chamber, carrying their ruler's commands to the other explosive monsters.

"Soon, we will—" Oxus started to say, but before he could finish, an explosion rocked the foundation of the hive. "What was that?"

The creepers in the gathering chamber scurried about. Many shot out into the curving passages, searching for attackers, but they found none.

"What happened?" Oxus bellowed. "Someone tell me what caused that explosion. Where did it happen? I need information!" He glanced down at the charged creepers. "Generals, take your warriors to the openings of the hive and secure the entrances. One of you, go to the heart of the hive and make sure our most prized possession is safe."

The sparkling creepers ran out of the gathering chamber and shot into the tunnels, squads of warriors following close behind. Oxus followed one group that moved quickly into a wider tunnel that wove its way deeper underground. The path was lined with redstone torches, placed there by the occasional NPC foolish or unlucky enough to stumble upon the hive. These prisoners would be put to work and kept prisoner until their HP expired. In all their history, only one NPC had ever escaped, and that one had been so close to death that it was assumed the villager had perished up on the surface. The secret of the hive was paramount to the creepers' survival.

As they ran through the lit passage, the king thought about all the possible threats: maybe mad zombies, or skeletons vying for more power . . . or maybe even NPCs, though it would take a massive army of villagers to take over the hive.

They followed the passage until it curved around and led to a gigantic cave. It had taken hundreds and hundreds of creepers to make this cavern, using their very lives to carve it out. It was used to store the hive's treasure; nothing was more important.

The cave was maybe fifty blocks tall and another fifty blocks wide. There were no torches lighting the chamber, but it was well illuminated. That was because of the pools of lava that sat in the floor around the chamber. But Oxus could tell the chamber was brighter today than it usually was. On one wall, a flow of lava spilled out of a newly-made hole. A crater was carved out of the floor nearby, with a small pile of gunpowder at its center. The lava poured onto the cavern floor, then spread out into a wide pool. Sparks and ash jumped up into the air from the molten stone. Oxus could see that if the lava traveled only a little farther, it would reach their treasure, which would be disastrous.

"How did this happen?" Oxus hissed. "What caused this explosion?"

His sparkling blue general moved to the edge of the new lava pool, then down into the new crater. He picked up the pile of gunpowder that sat in the bottom, then climbed back up and added it to their treasure.

"What is that?" the creeper king asked.

"Gunpowder," the general replied.

"How did it get there?" Oxus asked.

"I don't know, maybe it was . . ." the general began, but started to glow bright. He paused for a moment, allowing his ignition process to recede, then continued, ". . . a rogue creeper, trying to. . ." he waited again, ". . . destroy the treasure."

"He must have been sent by Herobrine before he left the server," the king of the creepers mused. "Thankfully, the lava did not reach the hive treasure."

Oxus turned and glanced at the center of the chamber. A massive pile of gunpowder sat in the center of the floor: the hive's treasure. It was the gunpowder from every creeper that had given their life to carve the tunnels and chambers of the hive out of the stone of Minecraft. This was a marker of their sacrifice, a reminder to everyone that the hive was more important than the individual.

The rogue creepers wanted to destroy the gunpowder because that was all the rogues thought about: destruction, Oxus thought. If the lava had reached the gunpowder, it would have detonated and likely destroyed the entire hive. Oxus knew how lucky they had been here.

"Put guards at the entrances to the hive," the king of the creepers demanded. "We must protect ourselves from outsiders. Soon, it will be time for the creepers to rise up and take over the Overworld, but not yet. We must be ready and we must be strong."

As the green-and-black creatures scurried off to deliver his orders, Oxus stared at the pile of gunpowder and breathed a sigh of relief. This gray mound was their most sacred of possessions, and the creeper king would do anything necessary to keep it safe, even if it meant going to war with the other monsters, or even the NPCs of the Overworld. But would it come to that?

CHAPTER 9

SURROUNDED

After traveling through the burned-out taiga forest, the party of NPCs finally reached a desert biome. As it was another wasteland, it offered little to look at, but at least it was alive. Gameknight felt like he could still taste the ash on his tongue, and drinking water didn't seem to help. The black dust had seemed to coat everything as they moved through the burned forest. It was a welcome relief to have the smell of ash finally removed from their noses, replaced by the warm, dry odors of the desert.

As they rode, Gameknight heard the sounds of splashing water. But before he could say anything, Butch was leading them toward it, over a sandy hill to a nearby stream. The horses eagerly waded into the tiny river, washing all the ash and soot from their legs. The wolves took to the water instantly, their fur having become sooty and black. They clearly did not like having the dead remains of that forest all over them, and were happy to be snowy white once again.

The washing in the stream buoyed all of their spirits, as did the signs of life in the desert. Tall, green sugar cane grew in patches along the bank of the stream. Their thin stalks stretched high into the sky like living green ladders without the rungs. Tall, prickly cactus dotted the landscape as well, their lush, green skin beautiful compared to the ashen, gray land the group had just traversed.

At dawn, the party moved from the desert into a savannah. Gameknight loved the sight of the twisted acacia trees, their unique trunks bending and curving toward the sky. They paused for a moment in the hot environment to rest and eat. Gameknight found a large tree and dismounted. Tying his horse to the angular trunk, he sat down in the shade and took out an apple and some pork. The horse seemed grateful for the respite and hung his head down low to munch on the gray-green grass.

Looking about, he could see all of his companions under a different tree, relaxing in the shade, with the exception of Butch. The big NPC had ridden up a hill and surveyed their surroundings, searching for threats. It seemed unnecessary, as Herder's wolves were out there patrolling already, and nothing could get past their lupine eyes and ears.

"Doesn't he ever get tired?" Hunter asked, gesturing to Butch with a loaf of bread in her hand.

"Apparently not," Stitcher replied. "He needs to slow down and rest, or he'll fall apart."

"He doesn't need to rest," Hunter added. "All he needs is to destroy monsters. That's what he feeds on now: destruction."

"That doesn't seem very sustainable," Crafter said. "His body still needs nourishment."

"You'd be surprised how long hate and revenge can keep you going," Hunter murmured.

"Hmm," Crafter said as he stared up at the big NPC, lost in thought.

"Hey, where's Herder?" Digger suddenly asked.

The stocky NPC stood, a worried look on his face. Gameknight also got up, then mounted his weary horse. Kicking the steed into a gallop, he began to ride in a wide circle around the group, searching for his lanky friend. Just as he was about half-way around the party, he spotted Herder, riding toward them with a string of horses obediently following close behind. Four wolves ran alongside the animals, their keen eyes always scanning the terrain for monsters. When he saw Gameknight, the lanky boy sat up tall in the saddle and waved.

"Hi, Gameknight," the boy said with a grin.

Shaking his head, the User-that-is-not-a-user had no choice but to smile in relief.

"Where have you been, Herder?"

"I figured we needed fresh horses, so I went out and got some."

"You just went out into the wilderness, alone, to find horses?" Gameknight clarified.

Herder shook his boxy head as he drew up to his friend's side, his long, black hair falling across his face.

"I wasn't alone!" Herder replied. "I had some wolves with me."

"Wolves!" Gameknight exclaimed. "You only have four of them with you. What if you had run into a large group of monsters?"

"If they had sensed any monsters, then they would have called the other wolves to come help,"

Herder explained. "There was no danger, but it's nice that you're worried about me."

The young boy rode past Gameknight999 and headed back to their companions. As he drew closer to the others, he motioned to the horses to come to him. One by one, he assigned each animal to a rider. Gameknight ended up with a white-spotted, gray horse with a black mane. His black-and-white horse seemed happy to have the saddle off its back and quickly wandered away in case Gameknight changed his mind. Somehow, Herder had tamed all the horses, so he didn't need to do anything other than place the saddle on its back and mount. Strong muscles rippled within his new horse's boxy form as Gameknight kicked it into a trot. This was a strong animal, the kind you would want with you in battle; she was a warhorse.

Though she was the wrong color, Gameknight decided he would name this horse after the most famous one he could think of. "I shall name you Trigger . . . that OK, girl?"

The horse whinnied and tossed her head, her black mane flipping from the left to the right.

"OK, then," Gameknight said. "Trigger it is."

He spun in a tight circle, looking at his comrades. They all had their new horses saddled and were releasing their weary ones back into the wild.

"Let's get moving," the User-that-is-not-a-user said. "If we keep going, we will—"

"We ride hard from here on out," Butch interrupted. "We'll get to Crafter's village by dark if you all keep up with me."

The others nodded and urged their horses forward, following Butch. Gameknight just sat there in shock.

I was just saying something, and Butch talked right over me, Gameknight thought. *But what's worse, everyone just followed him and ignored me. Do they even care that I'm here?*

One of the wolves barked. Turning, he saw one of the animals bringing up the rear staring at him, the wolf's black eyes filled with restless impatience.

"Yeah, yeah . . . I'm coming," Gameknight said.

He kicked his horse into a gallop and caught up with the party.

By noon, they had made it to the other side of the savannah. Ahead of them was a plains biome; the thick, lush grass would be inviting to the horses. Right next to this biome was an oak forest. The tall trees offered shade and would make the journey much easier. The party rode along the border of the two biomes, staying in the forest biome when possible, but also diverting to the grassland to allow the horses to eat.

After an hour of an easy gallop, one of the wolves stopped in their tracks and started to howl. The other wolves then did the same, howling and growling at the constant east-to-west breeze, as if it carried with it some kind of threat.

And then Gameknight smelled it . . . smoke.

"There's a fire somewhere," he said.

"This way, come on!" Butch cried as he kicked his horse into a gallop.

The big NPC shot to a nearby hill. When he reached the top, he skidded to a stop and glanced around. Gameknight streaked up the hillside, then gazed around at their surroundings. Near the edge of the forest, a column of smoke rose into the air, the black cubes forming billowing and ominous shapes. An angry glow encircled the bottom of the smoke, and it was growing brighter. Near the fire was a village ringed in a cobblestone wall. From this distance, Gameknight couldn't see any activity, but he could imagine the fear surging through the villagers at the sight of the flames.

"Everyone, this way!" Butch shouted. "We need to stop the blazes before they destroy the entire forest."

Without waiting for a response, Butch's horse leapt forward, directly toward the forest. Gameknight turned to look at Hunter, but she had already kicked her new horse into action, followed by the rest of the party. Only Herder remained on the hilltop at his side.

"Herder, take your wolves and go to the village," Gameknight said. "We'll need the villagers ready with buckets and water."

"But I can fight," Herder complained.

"I know, but if you go down there, your wolves will get hurt. It's more important that they go to the village and protect the NPCs. Besides, we will need that water if we're going to stop this fire. I'm counting on you."

Herder glanced at Butch and the other warriors charging toward the forest fire, then back at Gameknight.

"OK, I'm sure you know best," Herder said.

I'm glad someone *thinks so,* Gameknight thought.

Without delay, Herder nudged his horse with his heels and took off at a gallop toward the village, the snowy-white wolves loping at his side.

Gameknight then kicked his horse forward and charged after his friends. As he rode, he pulled out his enchanted bow and notched an arrow. The iridescent purple light coming from the magical weapon shone on the tip of the projectile, as if it was enchanted as well.

In thirty seconds, he'd cut the distance between him and his friends in half. And in another thirty seconds, he was riding next to Butch, his big gray horse easily outpacing all the other steeds.

Suddenly, an unnatural sound reached his ears, making tiny square goose bumps form on his arms and neck. It was a mechanical breathing sound, as if some kind of robotic monster was gasping for air. He instantly recognized the sound: blazes.

Gameknight charged into the hazy forest, searching for targets, but the black smoke became so thick as they neared flames it was impossible to see any of the monsters.

"I can't see anything!" Hunter said with a cough behind him.

"Me neither," Crafter added. "How are we going to fight these things if we can't see them?"

Gameknight scanned the smoke-filled forest, but he couldn't make out anything.

"Everyone, get out your swords and follow me," Butch said. "We're charging forward."

As usual, the big NPC didn't wait to see if anyone would follow. He charged ahead into the smoke, yelling at the top of his lungs. Hunter glanced at Gameknight, then shrugged and drew her sword as she charged after him. The rest of them followed her example and rode into the black clouds, swords held up high.

"No, you can't just charge out there!" Gameknight cried out to them, but nobody could hear him over the crackling of the flames.

Snapping the reins, he followed his friends, but kept his bow out instead of his blade. He knew they would never get close enough to the blazes to use a sword. After he'd moved a dozen blocks, he found a wall of flames blocking his path. Just beyond, he spotted his friends, all of them surrounded by the fire. Floating a few blocks above the flames were orange, glowing blazes lit up like bright golden lampposts on a foggy night. There were a lot of them, and they had completely surrounded his friends. They were trapped, and it was up to Gameknight999 to save them . . . somehow . . .

CHAPTER 10

THE PORTAL

"You should not be here!" one of the blazes thundered through the swirling clouds of smoke.

"We won't let you burn this forest down!" Butch screamed back. "Come down here and face your punishment."

The blaze laughed, making his internal flame glow bright.

The smoke shifted momentarily, and Gameknight could now see which one was talking. Drawing an arrow back, he fired, then drew another and fired again, and again. Three deadly missiles streaked toward the monster, their purple flames lighting the smoke with a blue glow. The arrows all struck the monster, causing it to flare bright for just an instant, then grow dark.

"Pull out your bows and fire!" Gameknight yelled.

Pulling out his hoe, he quickly extinguished the flames before him, creating an exit path from the ring of flame for his friends to escape through.

"Come on . . . this way," he said, and he put away the tool and drew his bow again.

Fireballs rained down upon his friends, but the smoke made it difficult for the blazes to see as well. The monsters' attack was focused on where they had heard Butch's voice, but he had already moved. The party was now streaking toward the break in the circle, firing as they rode. Gameknight held his position and added his arrows to the attack, sending three quick shots towards a blaze, then turning to find another target. Glowing blaze rods fell from the sky as he destroyed monster after monster.

Once they were all out of the trap, Gameknight sprinted for the edge of the forest to regroup. As he rode through the smoke, the User-that-is-not-a-user saw something he didn't understand: a rectangle of flame that undulated and pulsed, with sparkling yellow particles all around it. Blazes were flowing out of the rectangle as if it were a doorway to another dimension.

"A portal!" Gameknight exclaimed.

Kicking his horse into a gallop, he shot out of the smoke and rode to his friends.

"Crafter . . . I saw it," the User-that-is-not-a-user said.

"What are you talking about?" Crafter asked.

But before he could respond, Butch spoke.

"We have to go back in there and attack!"

"That worked really well last time," Hunter said, sarcastically. "This time we—"

But before she could finish her sentence, a scream cut across the grassy plain. Gameknight turned and saw flames licking up the sides of the village walls like hungry demons. Some of the wooden buildings within the walls crackled and smoked as flames bit into the vulnerable walls.

"The village is under attack!" Butch shouted.

Pulling on the reins, he galloped toward the screaming.

"Come on!" Gameknight added as he urged his horse into a gallop.

As he rode, the User-that-is-not-a-user could see blazes drifting up from the forest and heading toward the village. Behind him, the glow of the forest fire was getting brighter. Small, fiery explosions cut through the crackling of the flames as blazes launched their deadly fireballs onto the defenseless forest.

Ahead, Gameknight could see the same fireballs falling on the village. They tore great holes in the cobblestone wall as they melted through the barricade and exploded on the ground. As he approached the damaged wall, a thin boy could be seen on the ramparts. He poured a bucket of water down the cobblestone face. Blazes fired at the boy, but the lanky NPC was too fast, dodging this way and that as he pulled more pails of water out of his inventory and dumped them around the village.

Butch reached the village gates just a step before Gameknight. The wooden doors were already burned to the ground, allowing easy entrance to the village. It was a good thing there were no other monsters nearby.

As they arrived, Gameknight drew his bow and began firing. He took down two blazes before they even realized what was happening. Hunter and Stitcher both rode for the tall watchtower that sat next to the village's well. It loomed high over the community like a lone sentinel watching over the NPCs.

Smoke filled the air as wooden buildings were consumed in flames. Villagers were running everywhere, each with a bucket in their stubby hands, trying desperately to extinguish the flames.

Gameknight rode toward the fountain, then jumped off his horse and hit the ground running, his bow singing.

"Crafter, Digger, help the villagers put out the flames," Gameknight said. "Do what I did at the last village and pour water over the buildings. Get the other villagers to help."

The two NPCs did not reply; they just went into action. Organizing the NPCs into bucket brigades, they moved the water from building to building as Digger built steps up to the rooftops.

The User-that-is-not-a-user turned away and focused on the blazes again. Firing as fast as he could, he took down blaze after blaze while balls of fire streaked toward him. But then the monsters turned their fire away from Gameknight to focus on a figure charging at them from atop the fortified wall. It was Butch. He had his sword out and was yelling at the top of his lungs.

Gameknight999 steadied himself and fired at the closest blaze. His third arrow left the bow before the first had even struck home. In a few seconds, the blaze disappeared, its blaze rods falling to the ground. He then fired at another monster while he ran for the stairs that led to the top of the wall.

"Butch, get back here!" the User-that-is-not-a-user screamed.

But the big NPC ignored him, as usual.

Charging up the stairs, Gameknight reached the top of the wall just as a blaze flared bright with flame. Firing quickly, his arrow knocked the blaze aside, causing the volley of three fireballs to miss their target. Butch ran at the closest monster and leapt high into the air. His sword hit the lower blaze rod of the monster, causing it to flash red. Instantly, the flaming creature floated up higher, then fired straight down at Butch. Gameknight sprinted to the NPC's side, then jumped. He pulled out his large rectangular shield and landed on Butch with a thud, his shield held over both of them. The fireballs smashed into the shield with the force of a giant's hammer, almost knocking it from his grip, but the missiles were deflected away. The center of the shield began to glow as the heat tore away at the material. It almost grew too hot to hold, but Gameknight clenched his fist tightly and held on for his life. He knew if the shield were dropped, they were both dead.

After the last fireball fell, Gameknight dropped the shield and pulled out his bow. At the same time, Butch pushed him aside and charged at the blazes. The monsters had drawn closer to see what had happened to their latest victims. They did not expect anyone to emerge from behind the wall of flame they had created. Butch attacked the first blaze, while Gameknight fired his enchanted bow at another. Arrows streaked out from the cobblestone watchtower, striking more of the monsters.

Suddenly, the confident blazes, thinking they would easily wipe this village off the map, were being attacked from all sides. More arrows rushed up from the ground as the villagers dropped their buckets of water and fought back.

The flaming monsters tried to retreat, but they were too slow. Flaming arrows hit them from above as normal arrows pierced their internal flames from the ground. Those that tried to move closer to the wall were met by Butch's blade. In minutes, the remaining attackers were destroyed, and the village, though still burning, was safe.

Gameknight reached down and picked up his shield. It was still smoldering and warm, but it had survived the ordeal. He looked up at Butch, expecting the big NPC to express his thanks to him, but the villager was lost in a haze of violence and revenge. Staring out from the wall at the distant forest, they could both see it was completely engulfed in flames, the bright glow likely visible all the way to the horizon.

"There's no way we'll be able to put out that forest fire," Gameknight said. "The forest is lost."

"We could have stopped them if we had more warriors," Butch grumbled.

"Are you kidding? You almost got everyone hurt in the forest!" Gameknight exclaimed. "You were completely surrounded and had no way to fight the blazes. You can't use swords against them—they just fly away."

"I did OK up here on the wall."

"What are you talking about? If I hadn't stopped those fireballs with my shield, you'd be a cooked butcher," Gameknight said.

"We just need to hit them hard where they won't expect it," Butch said, ignoring what the User-that-is-not-a-user had just said. "A huge attack, that's what we need. A single, massive attack that will take them all out at once and make the Overworld safe again."

"How do you expect to do that?" Gameknight asked. "You don't know where they will be."

Just then, applause and cheering rang out from the villagers below. Butch glanced down at the NPCs, then walked down the stairs that led to the ground, his sword held triumphantly over his head. NPCs rushed forward to pat Butch on the back, congratulating him on how he attacked the blazes with his sword. Gameknight stood there, confused.

"But he didn't do anything other than put himself and everyone else in a dangerous situation," the User-that-is-not-a-user mumbled.

No one heard him over the cheering. With a sigh, Gameknight put away his bow and shield and came down the stairs to join the celebration. When he reached the ground, he could hear Butch telling everyone about his plan.

"When we find them, we'll attack the blazes in force and destroy them," the big NPC explained.

Gameknight watched as the villagers all nodded their heads in agreement. But then one lone voice spoke up.

"But how will you know where to find the blazes?"

It was Herder. He was surrounded by his wolves, and still had an iron bucket in his hand.

"That's right," Crafter added. "We don't even know how they are getting into the Overworld."

"Well . . . ahh," Butch stammered.

"I know how they're getting here," Gameknight said.

All eyes swiveled to him.

"They are using a portal of some kind," he explained. "I saw it in the forest. It seemed like it was made of flames or something, but there was no obsidian. In fact, there was nothing surrounding it."

"You mean it was just floating there?" Butch asked, a hint of disbelief in his voice.

"Yeah, it was just floating there," Gameknight replied. "Blazes were coming out of it and moving into the forest."

"Why didn't you just destroy it?" Butch asked, his voice changing from disbelief to accusation.

"Destroy *what*?" Gameknight said. "There were no blocks to break. Besides, I had just saved all of you from the trap you had just fallen into, and we were running from the forest. You remember that?"

Butch just grunted.

Gameknight sighed and turned to face Crafter.

"We need to make a plan and figure out what to do with these blazes," Gameknight said. "We can't keep losing forest after forest."

"Yes, eventually it will throw everything out of balance," Crafter replied. "And Minecraft does not like being out of balance. Strange things can happen when the server is strained too much. I think we should—"

"We will return to Crafter's village," Butch announced. "Any warriors from this village that want to accompany us may do so. We'll be traveling by horseback so that we can protect more villages and forests on the way. The blazes will not stop us!"

He held his sword up high into the air, causing the villagers to cheer and raise their own weapons over their heads. Moving to his horse, which stood next to the village well, Butch swung up into the saddle. He raised his sword into the air again, causing more cheers to erupt.

"You have to hand it to him," a voice said from behind Gameknight.

He glanced over his shoulder and found Hunter standing close.

"People love his confidence and enthusiasm," she said. "They love a winner."

"But he's careless and reckless," Gameknight complained. "He's going to get people hurt, or worse."

"Perhaps," Hunter continued. "But right now, maybe the people need a symbol more than they need common sense."

"That symbol might get them all killed," he replied.

"Maybe. But at least now we know how the blazes are getting into the Overworld, thanks to you," she said. "And that's important. If we can close the other side of that portal, then maybe we don't need to fight a massive battle to win."

"But where is the other side of the blazes' portal?" Digger asked as he joined the conversation.

Gameknight999 shivered as a cold wave of fear slithered down his spine. He had a good idea where the portal led, but he did not want to go back there. No matter how big of an army they had . . . it would be dangerous, and many of them would not make it back alive.

CHAPTER II
REVENGE

Charybdis glared down at his general while his warriors returned through the fiery portal. Smoke from the forest fire was still streaming in behind them, filling the gathering chamber in the Nether fortress with luscious fumes and wonderful ash. The blaze king drew in a deep, wheezing breath. He could taste the destruction in his lungs . . . it was delicious.

"Is that village destroyed?" the blaze king asked.

The general floated backward until he bumped into the dark wall of the chamber. Nervously, he looked up at his king as he spoke in a raspy voice.

"It wasn't our fault," the general said. "The villagers fought back. They've never done that before."

Charybdis took in another breath as his internal flame grew bright with rage.

"They've always just cowered and hid when we attacked their villages," the blaze said defensively. "But for some reason, this time they had courage and leadership, and they fought back. Our blazes didn't stand a chance against all their arrows."

"I've told you a hundred times: always go after their crafter first!" the blaze king boomed. "He is their leader. Destroy him and the other villagers will just cower and do nothing while you destroy them."

"This blaze here was the only one to escape the village," the general said.

Charybdis stared down at a smaller blaze standing next to his general. He could tell that this warrior was weak, having been hit by multiple arrows while he escaped. If he didn't feed on some lava soon, he would likely perish. The blaze king could see fear on his fiery face—fear of his HP diminishing to zero, but also fear of what his king was going to do to him for failing.

I'll just let him worry for a while as to which fate would be worse, Charybdis thought with a smile.

"Tell me what you saw at the village," the king of the blazes commanded.

The young creature took in a strained breath and then spoke. "Some NPCs showed up after we started the attack. They were on horseback and rode in from across the plain. A couple of them had enchanted bows; their arrows had devastating effects." He stopped to draw another rasping breath. "But the real problem was the big NPC in iron armor. He charged right at us."

"Did he have one of these enchanted bows?" Charybdis asked.

"No, he had a sword."

"A SWORD!" screamed the blaze king. "How can a sword hurt you? All you have to do is rise up into the air and then bury the villagers with fireballs."

The blaze cowered a little more. His internal flame began to flicker and become unstable. He looked hungrily at a pool of lava on the other side of the gathering chamber, then turned his gaze back up at his king.

"We did that, Sire. We launched fireballs at the villager with the sword, but another came to his aid. He used a large, flat piece of wood and metal to protect him from our attack. Our fireballs had no effect."

"What happened next?" the king of the blazes asked.

"After the villager survived our attack, the other villagers rallied together and began firing on us with their bows. The one in charge gave the villagers courage. Only I was able to get away to bring you this news."

While talking, the blaze had slowly started to float toward the lava, hoping that Charybdis would not notice.

"There seems to be a puzzle here," the blaze king said, causing the weakened monster to stop in his tracks. "Do you have anything else to report?"

The blaze shook his head as his internal flame flickered and sputtered.

"Very well . . . go feed," Charybdis said.

The monster floated to the pool of lava and slowly lowered itself down into the boiling liquid. Instantly, the creature's internal flame grew bright as its HP became replenished.

"Is there anything else to report?" the blaze king asked the general.

"Yes, a small band of NPCs challenged us in the forest," the monster said. "They were caught in a trap and encircled within a wall of flames."

"So you destroyed them?" Charybdis asked with an evil grin.

The general sighed.

"No, they escaped. One of their comrades extinguished part of the flames and then fired at us with a bow. It surprised the blazes, and they escaped before we could respond."

"You mean they just walked out of your fire circle?" the king of the blazes asked.

"Well . . . no . . . they rode on horses," the general replied.

The flames that held Charybdis' blaze rods together flared bright with frustration. Slowly, he floated up into the air, then moved forward so that he was directly in front of the general.

"Are these the NPCs that saved the village?" Charybdis wheezed, his anger growing.

The general nodded his head, then lowered it to the ground.

The blaze king's flame grew brighter and brighter until it was white hot. He rose higher into the air so that all the other blazes in the gathering chamber had to strain their blaze rods to look up at him.

"General, you have disappointed me for the last time."

Charybdis flared bright, then launched three super-heated fireballs at the failed monster. The general didn't even bother to raise his head. The fireballs hit the monster and instantly took his HP down to zero. He disappeared with a puff of smoke as his blaze rods clattered to the ground.

Slowly, the blaze king's internal flame cooled, as did his rage.

"I hate incompetence!" Charybdis shrieked, his voice echoing off the dark Nether brick walls of the chamber. "We will continue to destroy the Overworld, despite my pathetic generals. When we have—"

"Sire," a young voice interrupted.

Charybdis stopped in mid-sentence, shocked that someone had dared to speak while he was addressing the chamber. Swiveling his gaze down to the offending blaze, the king found a young monster moving forward, a terrified expression on his glowing yellow head. This creature was likely so young that it didn't even have a wheeze to its breathing yet.

"You interrupted me, child. How dare you! I am Charybdis, the king of the blazes and I—"

"There is something else you should know about the last attack," the monster said meekly.

Charybdis grew bright with agitation.

"What is it?" he snapped.

"I disobeyed my orders and went on the raid," the young blaze said. "I just wanted to help destroy the Overworld like my older brothers. But now, my brothers are gone, destroyed at the village." He paused for a moment as his internal flame flickered with grief.

"Continue," Charybdis ordered.

The young blaze took in a large, silent breath, then he continued.

"I went through the portal and threw my own fireballs at the trees," the little blaze said. "They weren't very big or hot like the warrior's fireballs, but I wanted to help. I saw when the NPCs were trapped in the circle of flame. I also saw the one that broke the circle and saved the villagers."

"So what?" Charybdis snapped. "So you saw a villager . . . who cares? This discussion is annoying me."

"But Sire, I'd seen that person before, when you were battling him outside this fortress after the Maker was released from that tiny chest."

"What are you talking about?" the blaze king asked. "When Herobrine's XP was released from the ender chest, I was battling the User-that-is -not-a-user."

The tiny blaze nodded his head.

"Are you saying the one that saved the NPCs in the forest was . . . ?"

The blaze nodded again. "It was him. I saw the letters over his head, but there was no server thread. It was he. It was Gameknight999."

Charybdis gasped a wheezy gasp as his flame grew bright with thoughts of revenge.

"So the User-that-is-not-a-user is the one responsible for saving the villagers in the forest fire," the blaze king said, his voice crackling with hatred.

"He must be the one that saved the village as well," the young blaze said.

Charybdis nodded his head, then glared down at his subject.

"I'm sorry for disobeying your orders and not staying in the fortress," the smoky child said. "But I wanted to help."

"Have no fear. You did well, child," Charybdis said. "You will accompany the warriors on our campaign to destroy the Overworld. And if you see my friend, Gameknight999, you must tell me right away. He and I have a debt to settle, and this time, there will be no one to help him. All the monsters of Minecraft will celebrate when I destroy the User-that-is-not-a-user. And after that monumental victory, Minecraft will truly be ours."

The king of the blazes gave off an evil, mechanical laugh as his internal flamed glowed bright with the hatred of his enemy, Gameknight999.

CHAPTER 12
CREEPER RESPONSE

The chamber was massive, fifty to sixty blocks wide, with a ceiling that was thirty—possibly more—blocks tall. Torches adorned the walls, casting circles of illumination that drove back the shadows. At the center of the room was a tall throne, with steps leading up from all four sides. Atop the altar sat Oxus, the king of the creepers.

The creeper king stared down upon his subjects. They had congregated in the gathering hall to discuss the troubling events occurring across the Overworld. The creatures crowded near the tall throne, their bodies creating a green and black sea of color that covered the stone floor. Some of the monsters spoke to each other, their bodies hissing and glowing brightly as they started speaking, and then dimming after a few words to avoid detonation.

Oxus started to hiss and grow bright, capturing the attention of his subjects. When they were all peering up at him, he stopped his ignition and glanced down at the creeper before him, who had come to report what was happening on the surface of the Overworld.

"The forests burn," the creeper said to his king. "The blazes cause this." He paused for a moment to allow his ignition process to diminish, then continued. "They also attacked a village."

"Hmmm," Oxus, the creeper king, mused. "Those foolish blazes will enrage the NPCs and bring their wrath down upon them. They are idiots. What else did you learn?"

"The User-that-is-not-a-user," he paused, "is fighting against them." He paused again. "The villagers are organizing."

The creeper stopped speaking and stepped back. Oxus suspected the monster had more to say, but he understood the gist of his report. Gameknight999 was back on the server and was likely gathering the NPCs into a huge army. Oxus had watched this User-that-is-not-a-user many times as he tangled with the other monster kings. The outcome was always the same: a massive battle ending in Gameknight999 somehow tricking the monsters and destroying them. They always underestimated him.

"They never learn," Oxus said aloud to himself.

He didn't really care what the blazes did. They could torch every forest and village in the Overworld for all he cared. The creepers were safe in their hive, deep underground. They had coal to feed on and cool, peaceful tunnels and caves for raising their young. The troubles of the villagers and blazes did not interest the king of the creepers.

Oxus had learned, during the Great Zombie Invasion, that it was better to just stay out of the way while the other monsters fought it out with the villagers. Too many times, the creepers had been used as disposable explosive surprises against the NPCs. Oxus realized long ago that they could never survive in this role, though it was not an opinion that all creepers shared. The rogue creepers that had left the hive wanted to be a part of the violence, seeking out NPCs to destroy at the cost of their lives. *But they didn't realize that violence only resulted in more violence*, Oxus thought. Due to a century of the rogues attacking the unwary, creepers were now hunted and killed on sight by both villagers and users. The only way to survive was to stay in the shadows, until one day there were enough of them to destroy every last village. Then the creepers would truly be at peace.

"Where is the User-that-is-not-a-user now?" Oxus asked.

The creeper shook his head. "We do not know."

Oxus frowned.

"It is important to know where Gameknight999 and his friends are," the creeper king said. "I have always said that the creeper kingdom should stay hidden and away from the battles between NPCs and monsters, but I fear the blazes will enrage the villagers and send them after all monsters, including us. We do not want a massive army of NPCs and users coming to the Hive. That would be disastrous."

"They do not know where we are," hissed one of the creepers in the large gathering chamber.

Oxus cast his gaze at the monsters in the chamber. They all nodded their green heads, agreeing with the speaker. *What fools they are*, he thought.

"We cannot afford to assume that our location is still a secret," Oxus said, his voice growing in volume until it echoed off the rocky walls. "The

NPC that escaped long ago may have made it to a village. Those foolish NPCs write down everything they learn and share it through their libraries in the strongholds. We must hope for the best but prepare for the worst. Gameknight999 is the biggest threat to us, and the only way we can be prepared is if we know where he is at all times."

Oxus turned to one of his generals. The charged creeper sparkled with blue electricity, casting shimmering light on the cave wall. But the glow from the commander could not compete with that coming from Oxus. The blue and red sparks created a flickering glow that gave the creeper king an enchanted appearance.

"General, take out your scouts and search for the User-that-is-not-a-user. We must find his location and make sure he is not on his way toward the Hive. If you can get him alone, then destroy him, but do not let yourselves be spotted by the NPCs. Do you understand?"

The sparkling creeper bowed his head.

"Be quick, be quiet, and remain unseen," Oxus said. He then turned and faced the mass of creepers in the chamber. "For the Hive!" he shouted.

"FOR THE HIVE!" they all replied, each of them glowing bright as the chamber was filled with the sound of a hundred creepers hissing.

"Now go," Oxus commanded.

The general scurried out of the chamber, a large contingent of creepers trailing behind. He knew they would divide into groups of six and spread out across the Overworld, observing from the shadows. The king could only hope that they would find nothing. But if the NPCs did come their way, his creeper kingdom would defend themselves to the very end.

CHAPTER 13

THE TIDE ARRIVES

They had raced the sun for the rest of the afternoon, trying to get to Crafter's village before dusk. Thankfully, there were no forest fires on the way, but there was a gray, hazy cloud that hung over the land to the west. Gameknight suspected it was a sign that the blazes were erasing another biome from the face of Minecraft, leaving desolation in their wake. But it was too far away for them to do anything about it; even if they charged straight toward the haze, they would never be able to reach it before nightfall. Besides, with the constant east-to-west breeze, the haze could be coming from anywhere. There was no way to tell where the smoke originated.

But the presence of the smoky cloud put the group in a dark gloom. They could all feel the blazes slowly chipping away at the surface of Minecraft, methodically destroying small pieces here and there. They were ravaging the NPCs' land, and something had to be done. But first, they had to reach their home and make plans.

Gameknight breathed a sigh of relief when they crested the final rise and saw their village standing strong and majestic on the grassy plain. The tall cobblestone wall was dotted with torches, illuminating the area around the village and making any intruders easy to see. Thick blades of grass swayed back and forth in the gentle breeze, creating an almost hypnotic effect that calmed the User-that-is-not-a-user with their motion. Splashes of color peeked through the verdant grass; bright yellow, blue, and red flowers dotted the landscape like little colorful gems sewn into a green, velvety cloth. It was truly beautiful.

Surrounding the village and their slice of the grassy plains was a thick forest of oak and birch trees, their dark brown and white trunks in competition to see which could occupy the largest piece of the forest and receive the most sunlight. Small saplings sprouted up out of clearings, new plantings likely made by Treebrin, one of the light-crafters that lived in the village.

Light-crafters were creatures made by the Oracle to balance out the evildoings of Herobrine. Each light-crafter worked on a specific thing: Treebrin worked to improve the trees, Dirtbrin crafted the dirt, Woodbrin worked with the wood. Similarly, there were shadow-crafters that worked on Herobrine's side, improving the creatures that hid in the dark places of Minecraft. Creeperbrine strove to make the creepers more lethal; Zombiebrine tried to improve the zombies by making them stronger and more deadly; Lavabrine made the lava more terrifying. The two factions were always at war with each other, though their battles were fought through the creatures they crafted; it was like a war by proxy.

Two light-crafters lived in their village: Treebrin and Grassbrin. They had been on many adventures with Gameknight999 and Crafter and had seen their share of battles. Numerous lives had been saved by the two light-crafters; the duo used their crafting powers to help create obstacles and tangled growths that slowed attacking monster hordes. Recently, they had been pivotal in capturing and destroying Herobrine while he had been in dragon form. Looking now at what surrounded Crafter's village, Gameknight knew they were likely responsible for all the thick fields of grass and the new trees.

As they approached, shouts of warning could be heard from behind the tall stone wall. Warriors appeared atop the barricade, and flint-tipped arrows were pointed down at the party. But once they were recognized, the voices of alarm changed to cheers of celebration.

The iron doors slowly opened, allowing the party to enter the village just as the sun set below the horizon. Gameknight glanced to the west and could see the sky was shaded a blood-red, as if the atmosphere had been somehow stained . . . or wounded. The gray haze that now permeated the sky was lit up with the setting sun, creating an immaculate display of color and splendor. Normally, Gameknight999 would have stopped to appreciate the beauty of Minecraft, but the thing that was creating the magnificent sunset was the smoke from the dead forests and ash from the charred landscapes. It made him feel sick.

Stepping through the gates, Gameknight999 was greeted with cheers as the villagers celebrated their return. Filler and Topper, Digger's twin children, pushed their way through the crowd and jumped into their father's arms. As the stocky NPC hugged his kids, they both glanced over his strong shoulders at Gameknight999 and gave him a smile. It lit up his heart seeing their grinning young faces, and it reminded him of what they were all fighting for.

He gave them both a wink, then turned and searched for Crafter. The young NPC was standing next to Morgana, the witch that had moved into Gameknight's castle. They seemed deep in discussion, but the User-that-is-not-a-user needed to interrupt.

"Crafter, we need to tell everyone what is going on," Gameknight reminded him.

Crafter looked at the User-that-is-not-a-user and nodded. Reaching out, he grabbed a young boy and spoke quietly in his ear. The youth listened carefully, then ran off yelling, "GATHERING . . . GATHERING!"

Instantly, the villagers all began to move to the area around the central well. Mothers with children, workers from the crafting chamber, craftsmen in their homes . . . every facet of the community came to the water well to hear what Crafter had to say.

Crafter jumped up on the edge of the stone well and waited for everyone to approach. He held one hand up over his head, signaling for everyone to be quiet, while gripping one of the vertical wooden posts that supported the square roof overhead with the other. Some of the older NPCs and village elders moved through the crowd to stand on the ground near their leader, while the younger members stepped out of the way to make room. The User-that-is-not-a-user started to back out of the way, but Digger grabbed him by his armor and drew him closer; apparently, he was considered one of the elders.

Gameknight smiled.

"Quiet, please, we have much to discuss," Crafter said. "Things have been happening in Minecraft of which you must all be made aware.

"Tragedy strikes at Minecraft again. Forests burn out of control. Biomes are being made uninhabitable, and villagers are being attacked."

The NPCs murmured at this, some of them reaching for their swords and scanning the skies for threats.

"The blazes of the Nether are trying to burn everything and reduce the Overworld to ash and soot. The king of the blazes, Charybdis, has the monsters charring the very soil until it melts into shattered glass. The creatures of the Nether will make it so that the land can never support life again. This is a grave threat." Crafter paused for a moment to let everyone absorb this terrible information. "So far this village has been kept safe, but we must assume this tide of destruction will eventually crash upon our walls. We must be prepared for what is coming. I'm asking everyone to—"

"We need to go to the Nether and attack the monster king before the fires spread any farther!" Butch interrupted from the back of the crowd.

"No, that would be dangerous," Gameknight called out. "We are not prepared to go to the Nether."

"It's always dangerous to go to the Nether," Butch challenged. "But we cannot leave these monsters to go about the Overworld unchecked. We have villages and forest and animals to protect. We have friends and families that must be kept safe. The blazes destroyed multiple biomes right before our eyes, and we were powerless to do anything about it. The only way to stop these monsters is to annihilate their leader. We need to destroy the blaze king."

Gameknight glanced around at the villagers. He could see most had angry scowls creasing their unibrows. Many were muttering to each other, nodding their heads as they glanced at Butch, anger filling their eyes.

"Let's get 'em," someone growled.

"Destroy all the blazes!" yelled another.

Many of the villagers drew their weapons and held them over their heads. Some beat on their armor with the hilt of their swords, creating a rhythmical *BANG . . . BANG . . . BANG*. The sound reminded Gameknight999 of a funeral drum . . . but if that was the case, whose funeral was it?

"Exterminate them all! What are we waiting for? Let's go!" Butch yelled.

The villagers were getting whipped up into a frenzy, feeding on the anger and hate that Butch was serving up.

Even the villagers listen to Butch instead of me, Gameknight thought.

He sighed.

"At least we should wait and prepare," Gameknight said in a loud voice, trying to be heard over Butch's cries for violence. "We need new armor and stronger weapons. Blazes are difficult enemies to battle. If you insist on going to the Nether, at least hold off until we're ready. Going off unprepared could cause a disaster."

"The User-that-is-not-a-user gives wise counsel," Crafter said in a loud voice that quieted the crowd. "We should prepare before traveling to the Nether to battle. It will take the blazes a long time to travel from their portal to our doorstep. There is time to craft new armor and weapons for the warriors."

"And fire resistance potions," Gameknight added. "Morgana, the witch that lives in my castle, can make many potions for us as long as we give her time. For once, we have time to prepare and move cautiously, instead of being driven by our foe. We should take advantage of the opportunity."

Some of the villagers nodded their heads, but many still frowned, hot anger burning from within.

"Gameknight is right," Crafter added. "Let us take time and prepare, so that we can be victorious."

Butch seemed disappointed as the villagers nodded and put away their weapons.

"We will first—"

"FIRE!" shouted the watcher from atop the tall cobblestone watchtower.

Everyone turned their heads up to the voice. Watcher was pointing toward the forest with his iron sword.

Gameknight ran for the steps that led to the top of the fortified wall. As he ran, Butch blew past him, nudging him out of the way and climbing the stairs first.

When Gameknight reached the top of the battlement, he gasped at the sight of the forest that stood before the village. Tall pillars of smoke billowed up into the sky as bright orange flames danced across the top of the trees. Intense white balls of fire could be seen streaking through the forest, engulfing branches and trunks.

"It appears the time to wait and prepare has ended, and the time to act is now!" Butch said as he drew his sword and sprinted down the steps to the ground.

He then threw open the doors to the village and charged out toward the burning forest, a large group of warriors following close behind.

"Wait! You need fire resistance potions!" Gameknight yelled, but he could not be heard over the shouts and clanking of armor.

Suddenly, a blaze streaked out of the forest and launched a fireball at the village wall. The white-hot sphere crashed into the cobblestone and shattered it as if it were made of glass. Then more fireballs streaked out of the woods and smashed into the village, one setting the blacksmith's house aflame, while another hit the library. As Gameknight pulled out a bucket from his inventory and ran for the village well, he shook with fear. The tide of destruction had finally reached their shores, and they weren't ready . . . not at all.

CHAPTER 14

CIRCLE OF FLAME

Warriors ran out toward the burning forest, while others stayed behind to fight the fires in the village. Gameknight999 ran to the village well and filled three buckets with water, then dashed to the library. Jumping into the air, he placed blocks of dirt under his feet as he climbed upward. When he reached the height of the roof, the User-that-is-not-a-user dumped the water on top of the library. The blue liquid spread across the building and quickly extinguished the flames.

He tossed the buckets to a villager below, then leapt off the roof, taking a little damage when he landed. He didn't care. Out beyond the village walls, Gameknight could hear explosions from the forest, and more smoke crept slowly up into the air.

Something bright orange flared off to the right. Turning, he saw a fireball streaking straight toward him. Out of pure reflex, Gameknight999 drew his diamond sword and swung at the fireball just as it was about to hit. The burning sphere bounced off the crystalline blade and shot back toward the source.

It smashed into the blaze, making it flash red with damage. Before he could speak, arrows shot up from the ground, striking the confused blaze multiple times. It disappeared as its HP was consumed.

He looked across the village. Four other homes were on fire, with multiple smoking holes in the fortified wall. But thankfully, no more blazes were coming out of the forest . . . for now.

"Butch must be keeping them busy," a voice said next to him.

Glancing down, Gameknight found Stitcher at his side.

"Where's Hunter?" he asked.

"She is—" Stitcher stopped talking when a blaze floated above the cobblestone wall.

In a smooth, lightning-fast motion, she drew an arrow and fired, then again twice more. Gameknight also drew his bow and shot, though not as fast as his friend. Their arrows struck the monster, silencing its wheezing cries before it could launch an attack.

"She's out in the forest, fighting the monsters there," Stitcher said as she notched another arrow and scanned the sky.

Suddenly, a large group of blazes burst out of a dark cloud of smoke and headed straight for the village.

"To the walls—quick!" Gameknight shouted. "Anyone not fighting a fire, come with your bow and be ready."

The blazes were still far from the village, but they were closing fast. Gameknight knew they didn't have much time to prepare for this new assault. He sprinted for the stairs that led to the top of the cobblestone wall. But before he could ascend the steps, Morgana, the witch, was standing there, a devious smile on her wrinkled face.

"I have something for all of you," she said with a scratchy voice.

As NPCs moved past her, she gave each person two or three glass bottles. Gameknight peered down at the bottles and smiled.

"Clever," he said to her.

The old witch just glanced at him and then ran off on another task.

"Everyone, hide behind a block of stone and hold your fire," Gameknight said.

He crouched behind the rocky crenellations that ringed the top of the fortification. Glancing to his left and right, he could see all the villagers were doing the same, scrunching low behind the cobblestone blocks. He leaned forward and snuck a peek at the incoming monsters. They were maybe a dozen blocks away, and hadn't started firing yet.

"Not yet," Gameknight said.

He glanced at the other villagers and could see fear on their faces. They were all afraid of the blazes and their fiery balls of death.

They were now eight blocks away and closing fast.

"Don't be scared," the User-that-is-not-a-user said. "We'll wait until they're almost on top of us, then we'll attack."

He could see nervous glances from many of the villagers. Most of them were the very young or the very old; the majority of the stronger adults were out fighting in the forest. Gameknight knew that these were not warriors; they were grandparents and shopkeepers and children. But they were the only defenders the village had right now.

The blazes were only four blocks away.

"Ready . . . wait . . . wait . . . NOW!"

As one, the villagers all stood and started throwing splash bottles at the blazes. The bottles exploded on contact. But instead of a healing potion, or poison, or a potion of weakness, the splash bottles were just filled with water. The fragile containers burst on the glowing creatures, drenching the blazes. Their internal flames sputtered and dimmed. Some went out completely, while others barely flared back to life.

When all of the splash potions had been used, the villagers drew their bows and started to fire. Being so close, it was nearly impossible for the villagers to miss; unfortunately that was true for the blazes as well. Gameknight and Stitcher fired their enchanted bows as fast as they could draw arrows. Their flaming shafts pierced any of the blazes that seemed ready to launch an attack. In seconds, all the fiery monsters were destroyed.

"Everyone, help put out the rest of the fires in the village," Gameknight said before he turned to face Stitcher. "Come on, let's get out to the forest."

They ran down the stairs and streaked across the grassy plain. The occasional blaze drifted out of the smoky clouds and headed for the village, but they didn't last long. Gameknight and Stitcher fired just as each one floated out of the dark haze, multiple arrows striking the monster before it could even form a single fireball.

When they reached the edge of the forest, Gameknight was shocked by the destruction he saw. The glassy ground crunched under their feet as they walked through the burned-out landscape. Tree trunks lay on their side, their charred remains barely intact. It was like the scene of a terrible, horrific crime; words couldn't describe the devastation. Through the haze, they could see the glowing monsters floating high in the air, far out of reach of swords or axes. They glowed bright in the rising smoke, casting a brilliant orange circle in the sky. It was difficult to judge the distance, but Gameknight and Stitcher tried their best, firing arrows at the moving creatures of flame.

"I hit one!" Stitcher exclaimed.

"How can you tell?" Gameknight said as he coughed up what felt like a lung full of ash.

"They get dimmer for just an instant when the arrow hits," she explained.

The User-that-is-not-a-user watched as the young girl fired another arrow at the blaze. The monster flashed just before throwing a volley of fireballs, and then grew dim. She fired two more quick shots before it could move. The flaming arrows extinguished the monster's internal flame.

"There's more of them over here," Gameknight said, pointing. "Stay close so we don't get separated."

They moved off to the left, running past burning trees and smoldering patches of ground. Ahead, they could see a large group of blazes floating high off the ground. The smoke above the forest glowed a bright orange, lit by the monsters' flaming bodies. Radiant balls of fire streaked down to the ground, exploding on impact. Screams of pain sounded through the forest.

"Come on, there are NPCs out there," Stitcher said.

"Hold on. We need to go carefully and not just run into a trap," Gameknight said. "Follow me. I have an idea. Do you have any blocks of dirt with you?"

Stitcher nodded her head as she wiped ash from her eye.

"OK, come on."

Gameknight ran through the burning forest, careful to avoid any trees that were fully engulfed in flame. When they drew near the blazes, Gameknight found an oak tree that hadn't been set on fire yet.

"Stitcher, go to that tree over there," he said, gesturing to a nearby birch. "Climb up, but stay hidden. We need to get above the layer of smoke so we can see clearly."

Jumping into the air, Gameknight placed a block of dirt under his feet; he repeated the process again and again until he could climb into the leaves of the tree. With his axe, he carved a place out to stand on, with blocks of leaves still in front of him. Stepping up onto a green block, he peeked out across the top of the forest. Before him was a large collection of blazes, all of them launching their balls of fire at the ground. Occasionally, a flaming arrow would shoot up from the forest floor and strike one of the blazes, but not very often. There were so many balls of fire falling to the ground that the archers had little time for counterattacks.

"They have Hunter and the other villagers pinned down," Stitcher said as she drew an arrow back.

"Aim for the closest one," Gameknight said. "Shoot three arrows, then duck down, understand?"

She nodded.

"Ready . . . NOW!"

Stitcher fired her three arrows in quick succession as Gameknight did the same. They crouched immediately after the last arrow left their bowstring and listened. A loud clanking sound resonated in the air as the monsters took damage and then disappeared.

"Don't move," Gameknight said. "They'll be searching to see where the shots came from."

He stayed low and kept his ears open for any of the monsters. None drew near.

An arrow shot up from the ground and hit one of the blazes. It screamed in pain, then fired a shot back in return.

"Ready . . . AGAIN!" Gameknight instructed.

They sprung back up and let loose another quick three shots, each aiming at a different blaze, then ducked back down again as their arrows flew. Clanking sounds greeted their ears as the pointed shafts struck home.

Gameknight peeked around a leafy block. One of the blazes was coming in their direction. If it saw them, it would open fire and likely ignite the tree. They would be trapped.

"Get ready to jump," Gameknight said softly as he pointed to the ground.

Just then, a mechanical wheezing sound filled the air. The blaze was nearby, closer than he'd anticipated. He had to move . . . fast.

Suddenly, a flaming arrow streaked up from the ground and hit the blaze. The monster turned to face its attacker. This gave Stitcher the chance she needed. Standing back up, the young NPC fired a series of arrows into the blaze, extinguishing it.

Gameknight stood and fired three arrows at one of the blazes in the distance, then shifted targets to another and then another, not stopping to hide behind the leaves any longer. The blazes saw him in the tree and opened fire.

"Stitcher . . . JUMP!"

They leapt to the ground, taking damage when they hit.

"This way," Gameknight said. "Into the smoke. Put away your bow and enchanted armor. The smoke is so thick that they won't be able to see us."

They removed their armor and replaced it with mundane iron. With all their enchanted artifacts safely tucked away, the two warriors became shadows in the smoke, impossible to see. The User-that-is-not-a-user charged through the haze, Stitcher fast on his heels.

"Find another tree," Gameknight said. "We can do the—"

"DUCK!" Stitcher yelled before he had time to finish his thought.

The User-that-is-not-a-user hit the ground, just as a fireball streaked over his head. Stitcher pulled out her bow and fired three quick arrows at the attacking creature, making it disappear with a *pop*, its blaze rods falling to the ground like golden rain.

"That was a lone blaze, not one that was a part of the rest of the group," Stitcher said as Gameknight stood up.

"Thanks," he replied.

They found another pair of trees. Drawing their bows, they climbed into the leafy foliage and executed the same plan again, whittling down at the number of monsters that had their friends trapped. As the monsters' numbers decreased, the NPCs on the ground had more time to fire back at the airborne threats. With arrows coming from both sides, the remaining creatures were quickly overwhelmed and destroyed, leaving that section of the forest clear of blazes.

"Come on, they're over here," Stitcher called.

Gameknight notched an arrow and followed her. They put on their enchanted armor as they ran toward the sounds of their friends. When they reached the source, Gameknight found the NPCs trapped in a hole, fires smoldering all around them. With their hoes, the two companions extinguished the flames that surrounded the trapped villagers, then moved to the edge of the tiny cavern.

Hunter was the first to be helped out of the hole, her bow pointing skyward.

"They're gone," Stitcher said. "Are you all OK?"

The older sister said nothing. Soot and ash covered her face and smock. She watched the sky as the other NPCs escaped from the hole. Gameknight reached down and helped the villagers while Stitcher joined her sister, both of them standing guard and waiting to see if the blazes would return.

The last to leave the hole was Butch. The big NPC had his enchanted iron sword in his hand. He barely acknowledged Gameknight's help in getting him out of the hole. When the big NPC was free, Gameknight stared down into the pit and sighed. There were a dozen swords and bows and sets of armor left behind . . . maybe more. They had paid dearly in this battle.

He could see the ornately-carved wooden sword that young Builder liked to carry. He had been just a boy. And there was the elaborately-painted chest plate of Planter. She had just gotten married to Carver, and they were going to start a family. Then he saw Carver's bright red axe next to the colorful armor; they'd perished together.

People he knew had died here today and Gameknight had been powerless to stop it.

How can we stop these blazes? They're too strong, he thought. *Look at what they've done.*

"What happened?" Stitcher asked her sister.

"We were following the genius over here," she gestured to Butch. "In the smoke, we couldn't see the hole. We realized it was there when some of us in front fell in. We stopped to help them get out, and that's when the blazes showed up. The only cover from their fireballs was in the hole, so we all jumped in. Many NPCs never made it in . . . safely." She glanced down at the items that still floated at the bottom of the hole, then cast an angry glare up at Butch.

Staring down into the hole, Gameknight grew angry and sad, tears beginning to sting his eyes. He cast his gaze across the smoky remains of the forest. It looked like a scene from some horror show, the fallen trees twisted and distorted by the terrible heat that had destroyed them. Black soot covered the NPCs' faces like ashen funeral masks. They all peered down into the hole at the items of those that lost their lives. Some wept, their blocky tears carving out little rivers down their dirty cheeks, while others burned with rage.

Gameknight999 was so overwhelmed with sadness that his heart ached. He wanted to cry and scream at the same time. These were members of his Minecraft family, and they'd been destroyed by the blazes of the Nether—and for what? To burn down a forest? He had to stop this destruction . . . but how? The blazes were more powerful than he remembered, their fireballs hotter and more deadly. He knew if they went to the Nether, they wouldn't stand a chance.

Looking down at the enchanted bow in his hand, Gameknight shook his head.

How do I stop all this violence? he wondered.

The User-that-is-not-a-user slid his bow back into his inventory, but as he did, his hand brushed against something cool and smooth: one of the splash bottles. He held it out before him, the blue liquid within so clean and pure compared to their charred surroundings. The puzzle pieces started to tumble around in his head. There was a solution here . . . he could feel it. He just had to get past the grief and despair so he could see it clearly.

With a sigh, he wiped away the tears with a sooty sleeve, then turned and faced his friends.

"This was careless," the User-that-is-not-a-user said, his grief slowly being replaced by rage. "These were our—"

"They must be avenged!" Butch interjected as he stomped back and forth through the ashen remains of a birch tree. "The blazes fired on us without warning. They are criminals—no, they are rabid animals and must be put down. They took our friends from us, burned neighbors and family members, and we will not stop until every one of them are extinguished." Some of the villagers growled their agreement. "Everyone, back to the village so we can prepare for our counterattack."

The NPCs cheered, their eyes filled with rage at the destruction of their friends and neighbors.

"Back to the village!" Butch roared as he charged through the shadowy remains of the forest.

The NPCs ran after the big NPC, anger and hatred ruling their minds. As they bolted out of the village, Hunter and Stitcher stood at Gameknight's side.

"They're going to follow him again?" Stitcher asked. "He's reckless and dangerous."

"The villagers won't listen to me anymore," Gameknight said, lowering his head. "They will only listen to him."

"Perhaps they crave action right now, to satisfy their need for revenge," Hunter said. "I can understand that."

"You think they should follow Butch, huh?" Gameknight snapped. "He's going to get them killed with his rash desire to attack."

"I didn't say I thought it was a good idea. I only said I understand," Hunter replied.

"Well, we have to do something," Stitcher said. "We can't just let them go off into the Nether. They won't stand a chance, not against these blazes."

"Yes, we *have* to do something," Hunter confirmed.

Gameknight's heart was heavy. He felt unimportant and insignificant. But then he glanced back at the hole in the ground and saw the handle of a sword floating above a stone block.

Maybe they don't *listen to me anymore. Maybe I* am *unimportant in the villagers' eyes. But that doesn't matter,* Gameknight thought. *I'm going to save them, regardless.*

And as his heart was filled with hope, the puzzle pieces fell into place. Gameknight999 gazed up at his two friends and smiled.

"You have a plan, don't you?" Stitcher asked.

He nodded.

"I assume it's incredibly dangerous," Hunter said.

"Probably," Gameknight replied.

"I like it!" the older sister exclaimed.

"Then we better get moving," Stitcher said.

"Let's get back to the village . . . fast," Gameknight said. "We have an attack to delay."

The trio shot out of the ruined woods. As they ran, Gameknight could hear the soft music of Minecraft in the distance.

"Don't worry Minecraft," Gameknight said in a low voice. "I won't let you down."

CHAPTER 15

PREPARATIONS

When Gameknight entered the gates of the village, his ears were greeted with the sounds of despair. Wives cried for husbands that did not return from the torched forest; parents mourned the eternal loss of their children; friends wept for their missing neighbors. It was a level of grief that had not been known in this village for a long time.

Many looked to the User-that-is-not-a-user for answers—why had their loved ones been taken from them? But all he could do was put his arms around them and comfort them in their time of need.

"We must avenge our brothers and sisters," Butch ranted as he paced back and forth among the villagers, his sword held up over his head. "The blazes are trying to destroy the surface of Minecraft, and they must be stopped."

"Butch, we all know what the blazes are doing," Crafter said. "But we must also realize—"

"The *only* way to end this is to attack," Butch declared in a loud, booming voice. "We must go to the Nether. The blaze king is there. He must be destroyed."

NPCs cheered as their grief slowly morphed to rage.

"We can't go out there. We're unprepared," Hunter protested.

"No . . . we need to attack!" Butch shouted. "If you are afraid, you can stay behind."

"AFRAID?!" Hunter snapped. "I'm not afraid of anything, other than stupidity. Didn't you notice what just happened? Those blazes trapped us in that hole, and we couldn't get out. If there had been more of them, they could have gotten behind us and we all would have been goners. Without the help of Gameknight999 and my sister, we'd still be trapped . . . or worse."

"Butch, we need better armor and more potions," Gameknight said. "Without those, there is no chance for success."

"Those things will only slow us down unnecessarily. We have to go—now—and destroy them," Butch said.

"At what cost?" Crafter asked. His wise voice calmed the NPC mob. "Gameknight speaks the truth. Now is the time for preparations, not attack. We need a plan that involves something more than charging straight into the Nether."

"That's right," Stitcher agreed. "Gameknight, do you have any ideas?"

Before he could answer, Butch butted in.

"We will get the NPCs from neighboring villages," Butch said. "They will increase our numbers so that we can overwhelm the blazes. We'll then get new armor and weapons made, and stock up on arrows so that we can shoot the blazes from far away."

"There are other mysteries here to consider," Crafter said.

Some of the NPCs nodded their boxy heads.

"Gameknight, you saw the blaze portal a day's ride from here," Crafter said. "Blazes can't move faster than a horse. So how did the blazes get here so fast?"

"I don't know," the User-that-is-not-a-user replied.

"And how is it that their fireballs are so much hotter than normal?" Stitcher asked. "Look at our cobblestone wall . . . the balls of fire went right through it. How is that possible?"

"I don't know that either," Gameknight answered. "But what I do know is that arrows and swords are not going to defeat the blazes. We need something else."

"What else is there?" Butch asked as he rolled his eyes.

Many of the villagers began to talk all at once, some murmuring then glancing toward Gameknight999.

"Potions. We need splash potions so that we can protect each other while we're fighting the monsters of the Nether," the User-that-is-not-a-user said. "Without fire resistance potions, we won't stand a chance against those super-hot fireballs. Just ask the villagers that didn't return from the forest."

This last comment cut like a knife through butter. The NPCs now turned their eyes toward Gameknight999, many nodding their heads.

"Morgana can make fire resistance potions for us," the User-that-is-not-a-user explained. "We can each carry a couple of splash potions and use them on ourselves or on those around us. If we see someone taking damage, we can hit them with a potion and keep them safe. This will give us the edge we need to survive a battle with the blaze king."

More NPCs nodded their square heads.

"Where is Morgana?" Crafter asked.

"Here," she replied with a scratchy, aged voice.

The old witch stood near the tunnel that led from the village to Gameknight's castle. Her purple smock was stained and dirty, likely from the ingredients used in her many brewing stations. Her hat, like a black triangle, sat askew on her head as she stared back at Crafter.

"Can you make the potions we need?" Gameknight asked. "Do you have all the ingredients you need?"

"I have everything except for one thing," she replied.

"What's that?" Crafter asked. "Name it and it will be given."

"I don't think it'll be that easy to find," the old woman warned.

"Tell us what you need, witch . . . now!" Butch commanded with a hint of disgust.

Morgana glared at Butch as she reached into her smock and withdrew a splash potion of poison.

"You might need a lesson in politeness," the witch growled.

Butch took a step toward her, but Gameknight quickly moved between them.

"Morgana, what is it that you need to give us the splash potions?" Gameknight asked.

"Gunpowder," she said. "All the gunpowder has been used up to make TNT. There is none left in the storerooms. Without gunpowder, you can't have splash potions."

"Then just give us the regular potions, and we'll drink them right before the battle," Butch said, his tone still disrespectful.

This time, Morgana was the one to take a step forward.

"You should watch your tone," she chided.

Butch growled, but then grew silent as Stitcher laid a calming hand on the big NPC's sword arm.

"They must be splash potions," Gameknight said. "If you've ever been in battle and tried to drink a potion, you know how hard it is. You have to put away your sword and then pull out the potion, then drink it while you are being attacked. It doesn't work very well, especially if you have fireballs falling down upon your head. No, it has to be splash potions, so that we can throw them onto each other when we're in trouble. We need the gunpowder." He turned and faced Crafter. "Where can we get lots of it?"

"The only way to get gunpowder is to destroy a creeper," Hunter said. "I'm all for going after creepers, but I fear it will take us a long time to find enough to be useful. We may have to do this without the gunpowder."

"No, we *must* have it!" Gameknight exclaimed.

"Maybe there is another way . . ." Crafter said, scratching his chin and thinking.

"What do you mean?" Gameknight asked.

The young NPC didn't answer. Instead, he scanned the crowd until he found a specific NPC.

"Bookman, did the library survive the fires?" Crafter asked.

"Yes," the librarian answered. "Gameknight put out the fires himself."

"Excellent. Come with me," Crafter said as he ran toward the library, Bookman right on his heels.

In a few minutes, the pair returned. Crafter was carrying a book that looked like the ones Gameknight had seen in the stronghold libraries: an old, leather-bound tome that was dusty and worn.

"Crafter, what is that?" Herder asked.

"It was copied from one of the stronghold libraries," Crafter explained. "We all know the books in those libraries cannot be removed from the underground strongholds, so they must be copied in order to have them in the village's library. I remember reading this one when I was just a child."

He opened it and turned to a specific page.

"It is the story from someone a long time ago, who said they found an underground creeper village, where all the creepers live," Crafter said.

"Who was this person?" Hunter asked.

"Let's see . . . her name was Archer, and she was captured by creepers," Crafter said. "It says she was forced to work for them, digging and excavating with other NPC slaves, but she was able to escape. She barely made it back to a nearby village. They recorded her story, then put the writing in the stronghold library."

"Does it say where the creeper hive is located?" Stitcher asked.

"Let me see . . ." he skimmed through the text until he found the end of the passage. "It says the creeper hive is deep underground. 'The creeper hive is hidden under a mountain of flame where the lava meets the sea.'"

"I know where that is!" Digger exclaimed. "There's a volcano right on the coast. It is continually burning and smoking, with a constant flow of lava that spills down the side and pours into the ocean. The hive must be under that volcano."

"Then we need to find that creeper hive and destroy lots of creepers in order to get their gunpowder?" Digger said.

"No, there may be another way," Crafter said. "We can get our gunpowder if we can stay undetected. In the creeper hive, there lies a pile of gunpowder bigger than anything anyone has ever seen . . . at least that is how the legend goes."

"Nobody goes into a creeper hive and survives," Hunter said. "Even I'm not crazy enough to do that. Creeper hives equal certain death. They probably have millions of tunnels that go in all different directions."

"But that's where the gunpowder is, so that's where we have to go," Gameknight said.

"I'm not going on this pointless adventure," Butch huffed. "I'm going to the Nether, and I'm going to attack this blaze king and destroy him."

"You won't stand a chance," Gameknight said. "You remember how many blazes they have down there? We don't have a wither to help us this time, nor do we have an army of users to show up right when we need them." Gameknight paused as he scanned the faces around him. "No one in the physical world knows I'm down here this time. It's late at night, and everyone's asleep at my house. We're on our own. If you go to the Nether, it will cause the deaths of everyone with you."

"I am not afraid, nor are the warriors in this great village," Butch said. He paused as he considered his options. "But we will wait for you and your gunpowder as we make new weapons and armor. However, we will not wait long. The blazes are likely still trying to destroy more forests and villages. We must act soon, before it is too late."

Gameknight again scanned the faces of the villagers. He could see most of them staring at Butch, ready to follow him anywhere.

There was a time when they looked at me like that, Gameknight thought. *I used to be important, but now I feel insignificant, like a bug in Butch's shadow.*

"It doesn't matter," Gameknight muttered. "I have to do what I think is right."

"What?" Hunter asked next to him.

"Nothing," he replied. "Let's go get us some gunpowder."

CHAPTER 16

THE MONSTER SCHEME

The king of the blazes flared bright with rage.

"What do you mean, 'The village still stands'?!" he screamed, his wheezing mechanical voice making him sound like an enraged robot. "My orders were to destroy everything. Instead, you return and tell me that not only did you *not* destroy the village, but you also lost twenty-five blazes to the villagers."

"We did not expect the villagers to fight back," the blaze general said. "In all the other villages, the NPCs just cringed and cried out in fear while we destroyed everything around them. This time it was different. This time they weren't afraid to fight back."

"Excuses will not get the job done," Charybdis wheezed, his eyes glowing with annoyance. "I need results."

"But they charged toward us instead of away," the general said. "The NPCs in this village had courage and were not afraid of us like the others."

Charybdis rose from his throne and slowly settled to the ground; the blaze rods that formed his body glowed a bright orange as they spun around his internal flame. He settled directly in front of the generals, his eyes intense with rage.

"We must destroy that village," the blaze king wheezed. "Their spirit of defiance must not spread to the other villages. If it does, it could make our task more difficult."

"I will personally lead your blaze army against them right away," the general said.

"Not yet, you fool," Charybdis snapped. "We need a bigger army. It is important that they are all erased from the face of Minecraft. When you go to that village, you will have a hundred blazes with you. They will be so overwhelmed by the number of monsters under your command that the villagers will just drop their weapons and give in to their fate—destruction." He leaned closer to his commander. A white-hot ball of fire began to form under the king's body, ready to be launched. "I will not tolerate another failure. Do you understand?"

"Yes, I understand," the monster said, nodding his glowing head up and down vigorously.

"Now go and check on the blazes that are due to hatch."

"But that is a task for the lowliest of monsters," the general complained.

"That is your punishment for failing to destroy the village the first time!" the king of the blazes wheezed. "I want all blazes to see your humiliation. Maybe next time you won't fail me when I give you a command."

The general's blaze rods slowed their rotation around his central flame as his fire grew momentarily dim.

"Now GO!" Charybdis shouted. "Be thankful that I did not just destroy you for your incompetence."

"Yes, Sire . . . thank you," the general said in the meekest of mechanical voices, then turned and left the throne room. Charybdis laughed as the blaze floated out of the gathering chamber. The king then slowly rose into the hazy air and moved to a balcony that extended out of the side of his massive fortress.

Before him was the Nether's Great Lava Ocean. Rusty-red netherrack blocks stretched out in all directions. In many places, the blocks were burning, the flames forever alive and dancing over the ruddy blocks. Rivers of lava crisscrossed throughout the landscape, adding to the perpetual orange glow as the molten stone flowed lazily toward the ocean. In some places, lava fell from the rocky ceiling, splashing down and creating wide pools or falling directly into the ocean.

He could see the idiotic zombie-pigmen patrolling the area. They were useless; they wouldn't raise an alarm unless one of the invaders accidently bumped into them. High overhead, the feline-like cries of the ghasts filled the air. Their pale white bodies and nine dangling tentacles stood out against the reddish-brown netherrack blocks that covered most of the Nether. The gigantic floating gasbags tended to stay near the ceilings and never strayed low where danger might show its face. Since the destruction of their king, Malacoda, the ghasts had been timid and afraid of everything in Minecraft.

One of the ghasts floated low over the lava ocean and allowed its tentacles to drag through the molten stone, feeding on the heat. Cat-like sounds came from the pale monster as its health increased. In the distance, the blaze king could just barely make out the scars under its two dark eyes; those tear-like markings were a punishment for deeds committed during the Great Zombie Invasion. All ghasts carried the marks . . . and the shame. But soon, their shame would be erased when the monsters of the Nether took over Minecraft. When Charybdis released lava all across the Overworld, then these ghasts would again be free to roam the skies. But that would not happen until the biomes overhead were destroyed and the NPCs were eradicated. Then the landscape could be properly changed from that terrible green color to something more suitable—like netherrack.

A blaze moved down the ornate steps that led out of the Nether fortress. Charybdis saw it was his general and laughed again at his humiliation. Blazes followed the shamed monster, watching his punishment carried out. Slowly, the commander waded into the lava until he disappeared beneath the orange glowing liquid.

Charybdis knew the general would find the floor of the great ocean covered in yellow eggs with splotches of gold on them—their hatching ground. Soon, his new blazes would emerge from their flaming bath and feed on the fires of the Great Lava Ocean. His new blazes would grow strong, and with the magic left by the Maker, they would be more dangerous than ever. His massive army of monsters would cover the Overworld with their balls of fire, destroying everything in their path.

The blaze king smiled, then began to laugh an evil, wheezing laugh as his internal flame grew bright with malicious joy.

CHAPTER 17

SEARCH FOR THE HIVE

After getting a little sleep through what was left of the night, the NPCs woke early in the morning and started to collect provisions: fresh horses, food, weapons, and, of course, new armor. All of their old armor was singed and cracked. Crafter went to considerable effort to repair their enchanted armor rather than replace it; the strong enchantments on the diamond plates would be a difficult loss. As they prepared, Herder disappeared down into the crafting chamber. When Gameknight went searching for him, the workers said he'd last been seen next to the minecart network, mumbling something about "special friends."

Confused, Gameknight nevertheless knew he couldn't spend too much time worrying about what his friend was up to. He returned to the surface to check on the others. But when he reached the village well, the gathering point for the expedition, he only found Hunter and Stitcher.

"Where are the rest of the warriors?" Gameknight asked.

"Butch," Hunter replied.

"What?"

"Butch convinced the other warriors that it was more important to stay here and prepare for the war with the blazes," Stitcher explained. "None of them are going with us."

"What about Crafter and Digger?" Gameknight asked.

"I thought it better if we stayed here and watched over things in the village," said a voice from behind them.

Gameknight turned and found Crafter walking toward him, a concerned expression on his face.

"What's this all about?" Gameknight complained. "We're heading to a place that apparently only one person in the history of Minecraft has ever returned from, and all the warriors are staying here?"

Crafter sighed.

"Does everyone just do what Butch says now?" Gameknight asked. "What about me? What about the User-that-is-not-a-user . . . does anyone remember him anymore?"

"I know you're frustrated, but tensions are really high," Crafter explained. "Now that the sun has risen, everyone can see the devastation out there in the forest. Peoples' tempers sort of boiled over at sunrise, and now they're really angry and ready for action."

"Are they going to the Nether?" Gameknight asked.

"No. I convinced them to wait for your return," Crafter answered. "But I don't know how long I can keep them here. Riders have been sent out through the minecart network to gather more NPCs and bring them here to increase the size of our force. But if they get enough troops before your return, they might just decide to leave for the Nether early."

"There aren't enough troops to battle those blazes without these potions. Don't they realize that?"

Crafter shook his head.

"I'll do what I can to keep them from leaving, but you have to hurry."

Just then, Digger came walking up with four horses in tow. Gameknight was happy to see his white-spotted gray mare. The others wanted new horses, but the User-that-is-not-a-user had become accustomed to Trigger and had opted to keep her for this journey.

Hunter and Stitcher both mounted and made their way to the village gates. Gameknight swung up into his saddle and gazed sadly down upon the lone black horse remaining without a rider, five large white splotches across its boxy frame. It was Herder's horse.

"Any idea where he is?" Gameknight asked.

"No one seems to know," Digger answered.

"You can't wait," Crafter said. "You have to get going. Speed is paramount in this venture. Do you understand?"

The User-that-is-not-a-user nodded, then pulled on the reins and headed for the village entrance. The three friends passed through the gates in a strained silence. Gameknight was frustrated that the warriors had abandoned them, but he was also concerned about Herder and his disappearance.

After crossing the wooden bridge, they turned their mounts away from the rising sun and headed west toward the volcano that sat on the other side of the horizon. With no delays, they would reach their destination in a day . . . maybe less, if they didn't run into any monsters.

Kicking their horses to a trot, they rode through the tall grass and examined the destruction to their left. The devastated forest still smoked in places, but for the most part the fires had been extinguished. Nothing stood in the biome other than the occasional stump, but even those were few. Now, with the smoke cleared, the beautiful forest biome looked like an ashen desert. Nothing moved, nothing was alive, and not a sound was heard from that wounded landscape. Whatever animals had been in the forest at the time of the attack had either fled or had been destroyed. Now, no living creature would want to set foot in that area again. It made Gameknight boil with anger, and he understood the rage that was driving the NPCs back at the village. Still, that was no reason to go running off to the Nether to face an enemy of unknown size.

Gameknight shook his head as he kicked his horse into a gallop, wanting to find this creeper hive quickly and return before it was too late.

Suddenly, the sound of howling wolves cut through the uncomfortable silence. The noise seemed to be coming from behind. Turning in his saddle, Gameknight glanced back. Sprinting out across the wooden bridge was Herder on his large black-and-white horse. Surrounding him were a dozen wolves, all of them howling a loud song of pride and strength. That was no surprise, but then Gameknight saw glimpses of some other creatures with them that were hard to see through the tall grass.

"Herder!" exclaimed Stitcher as she waved at her friend.

The lanky boy waved back as he approached. When he drew near, the wolves began to bark excitedly, but Gameknight heard another sound that he couldn't quite place. It was a high-pitched sound that seemed strangely familiar, but he wasn't sure where he'd heard it before. Then the animals were running around them, and Gameknight smiled as Herder stopped next to him.

"I see you brought some new friends," Gameknight said, laughing. "I'm quite surprised."

Herder gazed down at the ground, then back up at the User-that-is-not-a-user.

"What's the big surprise?" Herder asked. "I figured we'd need a little help, since we'll likely be surrounded by hundreds of creepers."

Around Herder's horse ran at least a dozen cats of different sizes and colors, their meows mixing with the barks of the wolves.

"I remembered that creepers are afraid of cats," Herder explained. "It seemed logical to go get a few."

"So you just took off to the jungle?" Hunter asked with a smile.

"Sure," Herder replied. "Why not?"

"Didn't you think it might be dangerous in the jungle all by yourself?" Stitcher asked.

"I wasn't by myself. I had my wolves with me."

"Of course!" Gameknight said, then laughed again. "Well, I'm glad you made it back in time. Your cats and wolves are a welcome addition to our small party. Now let's go. We have a creeper hive to find."

Kicking his horse forward, Gameknight took off in a gallop toward the west, the rising sun shining down on their backs. What none of them saw as they rode away was the mottled green-and-black creature hiding in the tall grass watching them, blue sparks shimmering across his body.

CHAPTER 18

VOLCANO

Ash clung to everything as the four companions rode through the charred wasteland. The wolves seemed to get the worst of it, their fur collecting the sooty remains of the forest like iron to magnets. Many of the cats wanted to stop and clean themselves. But Herder kept everyone moving, encouraging the cats to follow along at the same pace with a high-pitched whistle.

As they moved through the burned-out forest, Gameknight saw many piles of blaze rods on the ground around them. That was strange. The golden remains of the blazes were far from where any of their fighting had been. Had other villagers been fighting with the monsters from the Nether?

"Gameknight, look over here," Stitcher called out.

Steering his horse toward his friend, the User-that-is-not-a-user moved to her side. She had dismounted and was staring at a pile of something on the ground, the grime and grit making it difficult to identify. Stitcher took in a huge breath then blew the ash away, a dark puff billowing into the air. On the ground before them was a pile of snowballs, the icy spheres glistening in the morning light.

"Snowballs?" Gameknight999 asked, confused.

Stitcher glanced up at him, then turned and looked at her older sister.

"Whatever this is, we don't have time for it," Hunter said. "Let's keep moving."

The younger sister swung back up into the saddle and kicked her horse to a gallop; the rest of the group increased their speed to keep pace with her. After an hour, they made it through the dead forest and entered a cold taiga biome. Blazes had not attacked this biome yet, but being so close to Crafter's village, it was sure to be high on their list.

They shifted from a gallop to a sprint to make up some time. Soon, they came to a frozen icy river. Gameknight used his pickaxe to break through the top layer of ice so that they could get to the liquid below. Each of them took their turn jumping into the frigid waters. While they were washing the horses, Herder placed a block of wood on the ground and lit it with flint and steel. They then moved the animals near the fire to get warm after their chilly bath. The wolves eagerly jumped into the water to free the ash and soot from their fur, but the cats refused. Instead, they rolled around in the snow, cleaning as best as they could, bathing themselves with their pink tongues.

"Five minutes, then we get moving," Gameknight999 announced.

The others nodded as they rubbed their blocky hands together near the fire to get warm. They were all frozen, and the fire was a welcome relief. After the allotted five minutes, they mounted their horses. Herder leaned down and extinguished the fire, then followed Hunter as they continued to the west.

They rode through the frozen taiga in silence. Wolves howled at them through the trees, but Gameknight told Herder to keep his animals quiet. Stealth was likely their best advantage right now.

Following the spruce forest in the taiga was a desert hills biome. Gameknight always found it strange that a snowy environment could exist right next to the desert. Sheets of snow sat right up against scorching sand, and yet the temperature from the desert never seemed to bleed through into the taiga. It was just one of the strange and wonderful things about Minecraft.

As they moved through the desert, they all kept a keen eye out for monsters. Herder sent his wolves out away from the party, creating a protective ring of fangs and fur, while the cats always stayed close to their master. At one point, everyone turned as a bark was heard from one of the wolves to the right. A desert village was just barely visible through the haze, with a tall watchtower that stood high above the sandy buildings. They couldn't tell from this far away if there were villagers in the tower; it was just a blurry spire in the distance. But Gameknight knew they were in a hurry and couldn't stop and check on them; time was their enemy right now, and they had to keep moving.

The trek continued in uneasy silence for a couple of hours, all of the warriors continuously scanning the terrain for threats. It was odd that they had seen no creatures at all.

"I don't like this," Hunter said. "There should be a spider or creeper running around out here . . . but there's nothing. It doesn't seem natural."

"There are creatures out here," Herder said.

"Yeah, I know, your wolves and cats," Hunter replied. "That's not what I mean."

"I know what you mean, and you're wrong," Herder added.

"What are you talking about?" Gameknight asked.

"Creepers," Herder said.

"Where?!" Hunter snapped as she drew an arrow and notched it to her bow.

"Behind us . . . there's a group of them," Herder answered. "They've been following us for a while now. One of them is all sparkly and shiny."

"A charged creeper," Gameknight hissed.

They all turned in their saddles and glanced back.

"You can just barely see them," Herder said, "but they're back there. They have been staying far enough away so they can just barely see us, which means we can barely see them."

"I don't see anything," Hunter said, squinting.

"Me, neither," Stitcher added.

Gameknight strained his eyes, holding a hand over his brow to shield them from the sun. And then he saw it . . . a blue sparkle that looked like a flat sheet of lightning. The image shimmered for just an instant, then disappeared.

"I saw something. It must have been the charged creeper."

"What do we do?" Hunter asked. "I don't like having a bunch of monsters following us. Let's go get 'em."

"No, not out here in the open," Gameknight said. "They'll have too much time to start their ignition process. We need to trap them somehow. Let's just wait and be patient."

Hunter grunted her disapproval but turned back forward and continued to ride, glancing over her shoulder every other minute . . . watching. The presence of the monsters on their tail added an extra bit of tension to the group. They picked up the pace and shifted between a sprint and a gallop, hoping to add a little more distance between them and their pursuers.

They rode up and down the dunes as if they were sailing across ocean swells. Green, prickly cacti dotted the landscape like emerald sea serpents sticking their heads up out of the sandy waves. They added a refreshing splash of color to the pale surroundings, giving the harsh desert a sense of life and hope, something that had been lacking in the burned-out forest around Crafter's village.

The User-that-is-not-a-user drove the horses hard through the desert. He wanted to get to the hive and get this business completed as quickly as possible, and the open countryside made traveling easy and fast.

After another hour, the party finally left the desert and entered an extreme hills biome. Steep, stone cliffs and gravity-defying outcroppings covered the landscape, most of which were impossible to scale. But *up* was not their destination; the creepers would be underground, hidden in dark tunnels and passages. In Minecraft, for some reason, the extreme hills biomes always had extensive tunnel systems running through the roots of the mountains. Those tunnels would lead them to the creeper hive and the secret pile of gunpowder hidden under the surface of the Overworld.

Weaving their way between rocky peaks, the party moved cautiously through the terrain, the hilly landscape slowing their progress. They could see the blue of the ocean start to creep into view, the gentle waters stretching out until they met the blue sky. But as they rode through the rocky biome, the smell of ash grew stronger and bit the backs of their throats as they breathed. With no fires nearby, Gameknight knew there must be a large source of lava somewhere close.

Moving past a large hill of stone and dirt, Gameknight was shocked at what he saw. A massive mountain came into view, with one side lit bright orange. In the dimming light of dusk, they had no trouble seeing the terrain, for a massive flow of lava was coming down one side and spilling into the ocean.

"We have to go *into* that?" Hunter asked.

"If you have a better idea, I'm listening," Gameknight said.

"How are we going to find the correct passage that will lead into the creeper hive?" Stitcher asked.

"I don't know. We'll just have to search carefully," the User-that-is-not-a-user said.

"This is a *great* plan," Hunter said sarcastically with a scowl.

"LOOK OUT!" Herder yelled suddenly.

Gameknight pulled back on the reins of his horse, just in time to stop himself from falling into a deep hole. Steering around it, Gameknight moved to a safe distance, then stopped to wipe his brow.

"Thanks, Herder," he said to his friend. "I think you probably saved me and my horse from getting badly hurt."

The lanky NPC beamed with pride.

"You know, that would be a perfect place for an ambush," Hunter said.

Gameknight stared down at the hole and nodded his head. *If they could just get the creepers into the hole,* he thought, *they could pick them off with their bows.*

"How do we get them into the hole?" Stitcher asked.

"Bait?" Hunter suggested, staring at Gameknight with one side of her unibrow raised.

"You want me to go into the hole and wait for the creepers?" the User-that-is-not-a-user asked.

"Well—" Hunter started to reply, but was interrupted.

"My cats could get them into the hole," Herder said.

"What?" Hunter asked.

"Yep . . . they could do it," Herder said confidently. "Gameknight, you stand there on the other side of the hole. The creepers will come toward you, but my cats will make sure they all are trapped."

"You sure?" Gameknight asked. "I'll be standing out there in the open like a sitting duck."

"A sitting *what*?" Stitcher asked.

"A duck," Gameknight replied. "You know . . . *quack, quack, quack.*"

Hunter stared at him, then looked back to her sister and laughed. "I think he's losing it, for sure," she said.

Gameknight shrugged and dismounted. He moved to the spot Herder had pointed at, then pulled out a torch and placed it in the ground. With the darkening sky, the light from the torch cast a wide circle of illumination, making him easy to see.

"I hope all of you are going to be ready if this plan *doesn't* work," Gameknight said. "I don't look forward to fighting off two or three creepers at the same time. That's not my idea of fun."

"Whatever. Just quit your whining and stand there," Hunter said. She had moved behind a large mound of dirt and was hiding, ready to spring out. "Now be quiet. I can see them coming."

Gameknight999 moved next to the torch and stood there . . . waiting. He was sweating like crazy inside his armor and yet felt freezing cold at the same time. He'd fought two creepers at the same time before, but he knew you had to time it just right: you had to hit one while you moved away from the other to keep them from both igniting. And if there were more than two . . . then he might be in trouble.

In the distance, he could see a flickering blue light begin to fill the dark shadows stretching across the ground from the setting sun. He couldn't see it yet, but the light was growing bright and brighter. And then the creature stepped out from behind a hill of stone and grass. It was a charged creeper, just as he thought, colored the normal mottled green but with a layer of blue electricity dancing around its body. This monster had been struck by lightning sometime in its past, and that electrical energy stayed with it, magnifying its explosive power. Charged creepers were very dangerous.

The sparkling monster scurried straight toward Gameknight, and as it came forward, more of its kind emerged from behind the hill. He gasped as he counted at least nine of them, every one headed straight for him.

Drawing his sword, Gameknight stood there and waited, fear nibbling at the edges of his courage.

CHAPTER 19

INTO THE HIVE

The sparkling creeper moved slowly toward him, its black eyes filled with venomous hatred.

"We've been looking for you," the charged creeper said, a hiss accompanying every word.

Gameknight took a step back, shocked. The monster glowed bright with each word, as if it might detonate at any moment. He had assumed these creatures were not intelligent enough to speak, much less know who he was.

"Really?" the User-that-is-not-a-user replied slowly. "Well, uhhh . . . it's nice to be wanted?"

He half-expected a smile from the creature, but only received a scowl.

The monster's companions came forward. They were just regular creepers, with no electrical charges dancing along their skin, all looking identical from a distance. But as they neared, Gameknight could see small differences: a tilted eye here, a narrow mouth there. They were each as individual and unique as the villagers.

The monsters stopped at the edge of the sheer pit and glanced down. As the creepers stared down into the pit, the charged leader glared at Gameknight999.

"We are not stupid," the creeper hissed, then dimmed. "We will not fall in that hole."

Gameknight did not reply; he just smiled at the creature. This seemed to infuriate him a little.

"Go around," the creeper said. "Get him."

Half of the creepers moved to the right side of the hole as the other half moved to the left. Suddenly, a shrill whistle pierced the air, followed by loud meows and barks as Herder's cats and wolves charged out from the shadows. At the sound of the cats, all the creepers instantly froze in place, including the charged leader. Creepers have an inborn fear of cats that is overwhelming, and with the sound coming from all directions, they didn't know which way to run. When the cats ran into the circle of light cast by Gameknight's torch, the creepers instantly backed away. Unfortunately for the monsters, more cats were coming from both sides of the hole, herding them into the center.

First one monster fell into the four-block-deep hole, then another and another. One of the creepers tried to escape and run away, but the wolves quickly cornered the monster and drove it back with its brethren. One after another, the monsters fell into the hole until the charged creeper was the last to step back.

"In the hole, and I may let you live," Gameknight said, pointing down as he drew his two swords.

"I'm not a fool," the monster said with a hiss. "The User-that-is-not-a-user is our enemy." He paused again as his body dimmed. "You will not keep your word."

"Get in the hole, or meet my two swords," Gameknight replied.

"I would love that," the monster said. "Come closer."

But before Gameknight could move, a flaming arrow shot out of the shadows and struck the monster in the chest.

"Get into the hole . . . NOW!" Hunter yelled from the darkness.

The creeper turned to see where the voice came from, then brought his gaze back to Gameknight999. Another arrow shot out of the darkness and hit the creature in the shoulder.

"GET IN!" she shouted again.

"The next arrow will end your life," Gameknight999 said. "The choice is yours."

The charged creeper glared at him with such overwhelming hatred that the User-that-is-not-a-user thought the creeper might just detonate right then and there. But the creature did not explode. Instead, it stepped down into the hole. When it landed in the pit, the monster stared up at Gameknight.

The others stepped out of the shadows and came near the edge of the pit. Hunter and Stitcher put torches on the ground, then drew arrows and aimed into the pit.

"Wait," Gameknight said, holding up a sword for them to stop.

The sisters turned and glanced at him, confused.

"We will not kill them if we don't have to," he said.

"But they're creepers," Hunter said. "They should be exterminated."

"No, they're living creatures like you and me," Gameknight said. "They will not be murdered."

The sisters both sighed, then put away their bows. Herder looked at Gameknight and smiled.

"Now, you're going to tell me where the entrance is to your creeper hive," Gameknight said to the leader. "If you do, we will let you live."

"Why do you want to go into the Hive?" the charged creeper asked. "You will not survive." He paused to let his ignition process diminish. "No one survives the Hive, other than creepers." The creeper waited as he grew dimmer. Some of the other creepers seemed about to speak, but he shot them a warning glance and then continued. "Even zombies and skeletons have tried to penetrate our home . . . they did not live to tell the story."

"We have our own business in your hive," Hunter said. She pulled back the arrow and aimed it at the leader. "Tell us where the entrance is located and you live."

The charged creeper took a strained breath, its body glowing bright for just an instant and then dimming again.

"OK, I will tell you," he said in a strained, weak voice, then mumbled something that was too soft to be heard.

"What?" Hunter said.

Gameknight and his friends took a step closer.

"What did you say?" the User-that-is-not-a-user said.

He mumbled again, then slumped against the wall as if his health were failing.

They moved right up next to the edge of the hole and peered down into the darkness.

"Tell us!" Hunter snapped.

The charged creeper gazed up at the NPCs, and its downcast mouth seemed to smile. Then a hissing sound filled the air, and the monster started to glow bright.

"GET BACK!" Gameknight shouted.

He grabbed Herder's armor and pulled the NPC backward, diving away from the hole. Suddenly, the pit was filled with bright light as the charged creeper detonated. The explosion caused the other creepers to ignite, creating a cascade of blasts that shook the ground as if the very surface of Minecraft were trembling in fear.

When the explosions finally stopped, Gameknight slowly stood and approached the pit, which now was more like a massive impact crater from some kind of deep-space meteor. The hole was a dozen blocks wider and much deeper. The sheer, vertical walls were now jagged and sloped, allowing Gameknight to easily climb down. The pit was now masked in shadows, the bottom seeming to be an impossible distance away. On the blocks that made up the sloped walls, ten small piles of gunpowder floated off the ground, slowly moving up and down as if riding on unseen ocean swells. The User-that-is-not-a-user stepped up to the gray piles and let them move into his inventory. He was about to turn around, but his nose caught the smell of something peculiar . . . sulfur.

Gameknight stopped and inhaled.

"What are you doing?" Hunter asked. "Every monster in this biome will have heard that explosion. We need to get out of here."

"In a minute. I smell something that doesn't seem right," Gameknight said.

Just then, he felt one of Herder's cats rubbing against his leg, curiosity having drawn the feline into the crater. Glancing down, he found an orange-and-white tabby walking a figure eight around his legs, leaning his head in with each pass. Suddenly, the cat stopped and stared into the darkness at the bottom of the crater. It took a step forward, sniffed the air, and then arched its back and hissed at the shadows.

"What is it doing?" Gameknight asked. "Herder, what's going on?"

The lanky boy clambered down into the pit and stood next to Gameknight999. They stared inquisitively at the animal. Another of the cats climbed down into the hollow and stood next to the tabby. The black-and-white striped animal did the same as the orange one, arching its back and hissing at the darkness.

"They smell creepers," Herder said as he stepped carefully forward into the darkness.

Pulling a torch out of his inventory, Herder held it out before him. The illumination revealed a massive hole at the bottom of the crater, previously hidden in the darkness. The NPC placed the torch on the ground next to the opening, then lay down on his stomach and peered into the newly discovered chamber.

"It's a tunnel," Herder said. "The floor looks like it has been rubbed and polished by thousands of feet. This passage is old and well-used."

One of the cats moved next to the opening, then hissed at the tunnel, its fur sticking out straight. Herder reached out and gently stroked the animal's back, calming it. He then turned his head and glanced up at Gameknight999.

"This is it," Herder said.

"Ironic," Hunter said.

"What?" Stitcher asked.

"That charged creeper was willing to give its life to keep the location of the creeper hive secret," Hunter explained. "But in giving its life, the monster showed us the thing it was trying to protect!"

"Stitcher, make sure the horses are well-tied," Gameknight said, shaking his head. "We're going to need them when we leave this place."

The young girl nodded and went to check the animals.

Hunter jumped into the pit and moved to Gameknight's side.

"How do you want to play this?" the archer asked. "There will likely be tons of monsters down there. We need to be careful and smart. Getting trapped underground by hundreds of creepers isn't my idea of fun. Caution should be advised."

"You sound like Crafter," Gameknight said with a smile.

"OK, then, what do you think we should do next?" Hunter asked. "What's your plan?"

Gameknight moved next to the opening and peered down into the passage. There was no movement visible, but Hunter was right: there would be creepers down there . . . probably a lot of them.

A shiver rattled down his spine.

But then he thought about his friends in the village and all the other NPCs in the villages across Minecraft. They all needed help, whether they knew it or not. Gunpowder was the critical piece of the puzzle, and if they could get stacks of it from the creeper hive, then they would have enough splash potions to protect all the warriors. Then, just maybe, the NPCs would stand half a chance against these new blazes and their super-hot fireballs.

Gameknight knew they had no choice . . . they had to go into the hive.

"Well?" Hunter asked. "Are you just going to stand there, or are you going to tell me your plan?"

"My plan?"

"Yeah . . . what's your plan?" Hunter replied.

"This," the User-that-is-not-a-user said with a mischievous smile.

He then stepped forward and dropped into the dark passage.

CHAPTER 20

DIVERSION

They moved through the tunnels as quietly as their armor would allow. Gameknight had them all take off their enchanted armor and replace it with mundane metal coatings. The light from the enchantments shown like beacons in the dark tunnels, so they put away their enchanted weapons as well. Hunter was not happy—she always felt more comfortable with her magical bow in her hand.

"Hunter, it's for your own good," Stitcher said. "You know they'll see the light from it, and the last thing we need right now is to draw attention to ourselves."

"Yeah . . . I know," the older sister replied. "It's just that the regular bows are so boring and pathetic."

"I promise, if we do come across any creepers, you can take out your bow and shoot as many as you want," Gameknight said. "OK?"

"I guess," Hunter complained.

Gameknight smiled at Stitcher, then turned and continued through the passage, following the cats that led the way. The felines could smell the creepers from a distance, and knew which passages were empty and which were filled with deadly monsters.

"Gameknight, how do you know we won't run into a huge army of creepers in the tunnels?" Herder asked.

The boy was carrying a redstone torch. It gave off a ruddy glow that lit the area around them but cast very little light ahead or behind. The cats could see in the dark and avoided any holes that might exist in the tunnels, but Gameknight and the NPCs needed some light to see these potentially deadly obstacles. As they moved through the corridor, they passed smaller passages jutting off from the main one. The narrow tunnels led to small, empty rooms covered with dust. Likely, they had been abandoned for years and years.

"I figure, this treasure of theirs . . . if it is so valuable to them, then that's where most of the creepers will be," Gameknight explained. "Besides, with your cats, we'll have enough advance notice to keep our of their way. At least, that's my hope."

"Is that your plan?" Hunter asked. "Hope you can avoid the creepers until you get to their treasure room? That's a pretty pathetic plan."

"You have a better one?" Gameknight retorted.

"Sure. Mine was to gallop through these tunnels and shoot at creepers until we run out of creepers to shoot at," Hunter said with a smile.

"We don't have time for something like that," Gameknight said. "Besides, we don't necessarily want to destroy all of them."

"We don't?" Hunter replied.

"Hunterrrr," Stitcher chided.

One of the cats hissed, and everyone immediately fell silent. The sound of shuffling feet echoed off the stone walls, making it seem as if it were coming from all directions at once.

"Quick—in here," Gameknight whispered.

He pulled out a redstone torch and stood near the opening of a narrow room. Herder dashed inside, the animals running behind him obediently; Hunter and Stitcher followed close behind. Gameknight then backed into the small room and put away the redstone torch, plunging them into darkness.

"Move as far back as you can," Stitcher whispered.

"Herder, be sure those animals stay quiet," Gameknight said. "If they make a sound and give us away, we'll be trapped in here."

The User-that-is-not-a-user could hear the lanky NPC whispering something to the wolves and cats, then everything became still as a graveyard. Gameknight held his iron sword in his hand, ready. He'd have no choice but to attack if they came in the room. Sweat dripped off his brow, even though it was cool in the tunnels.

Shuffling feet sounded in the outer passage. He couldn't tell if it was just one creeper or many . . . and he didn't want to find out. Gripping his sword tighter, Gameknight steeled himself for battle. His heart rate quickened and his breathing came in short, jagged bursts.

And then, suddenly . . .

The creepers walked right by them. They didn't stop to investigate the dark room, and it was too dim to see the footprints in the dusty floor. Edging forward after the footsteps faded into the distance, Gameknight finally peeked out into the shadowy corridor. They were safe.

"Come on," Gameknight whispered as he pulled out a redstone torch. "That was really close!"

They moved through the dark passages with the cats right next to Gameknight, while the wolves stayed near the back by Herder. Three more times, the footsteps of approaching creepers forced the companions to scurry into side rooms at the last second. Each time, the explosive creatures just moved past, hurrying on to their destination.

"I'm worried we're going to get lost down here," Stitcher said as they passed an intersecting tunnel. "These passages twist and turn in every direction. I know the cats can lead us to where the creepers are congregating, but they can't lead us out."

"You're right," Gameknight said. "I didn't think of that. We need to leave a trail that we can follow back out."

"That's easy," Hunter said.

She pulled out her pickaxe and carved a single block out of the wall at ground level on the right side of the passage.

"We make these holes on the right, then follow them back out on the left," Hunter said with a self-satisfied smile.

"OK, then," Gameknight said. "One problem solved."

They continued forward, the cats choosing passages that had the strongest creeper scent; typically, that meant taking the tunnel that led downward, deeper into the bowels of Minecraft. As they continued, a scraping sound could be heard. At first, it was just the faintest of sounds, like that of an insect flying at the edge of hearing, but grew in volume as they descended. And then they came to the source.

A narrow passage shot off from the tunnel they'd been following. Gameknight peeked around the corner; a pool of lava lit the room with a soft orange. All along the walls, he could see small creepers facing the wall, chewing at the coal ore that lined the chamber. But these creepers didn't look like any creepers he'd ever seen before. They were smaller, but they also lacked the dark spots across their skin that larger and older creepers possessed. Instead of being green and blotchy-black, they were covered with white and grey spots, while only the largest of them had spots that were nearly black.

"This must be some kind of feeding chamber," Gameknight whispered.

"Close it off," Hunter said. "That's a lot of creepers, and I'd rather not have to deal with them."

Gameknight nodded, then pulled out a block of cobblestone. He placed it in the doorway, then put another block atop the first, closing off the passage.

"Happy now?" the User-that-is-not-a-user asked.

Hunter nodded her head, her curly red hair reflecting the light from the redstone torch.

"Let's get moving," Stitcher said as she gently shoved Gameknight forward.

They continued through the descending tunnel, passing more empty rooms . . . and then Gameknight figured it out. All the empty rooms were feeding chambers that had run out of coal and been abandoned!

As they crept through the passage, Gameknight noticed the ceiling begin to rise upward as the width of the tunnel increased. His instinct told him they were getting close, and when the cats began to hiss, his suspicions were confirmed. Ahead, the wide passage opened into a gigantic chamber. Inside, they could hear the shuffling of many feet. *This has to be it*, he thought.

Gameknight had Herder take the animals to one of the empty side rooms just outside the cavern, while he crept forward to the large cave. Peering in, he could see at least three hundred creepers milling about a large, gray pile of dust sitting in the center: the gunpowder treasure. He was shocked at the size of the mound. There was more than they could all carry . . . a lifetime's supply.

Off to the side, lava was spilling out of a wall and spreading across the floor. The molten stone came dangerously close to the gunpowder. If one single ember were to shoot up into the air and land on the pile of gunpowder, it would create such a massive explosion that it would devour the volcano that sat overhead and leave a crater that stretched all the way down to bedrock.

Looking around, Gameknight saw some of the charged creepers, their sparkling blue bodies standing out against the flow of mottled green monsters. But one of the electrified creatures appeared different from the rest, with not only blue but also red sparks. It was as if this creature were imbued with both electrical power *and* redstone power! The combination of the red and blue light gave the creeper a purple hue that seemed almost magical. Terrifyingly magical.

Gameknight withdrew and returned to where his friends were waiting.

"I saw the pile of gunpowder," Gameknight said. "It's more than we'll ever need. All we have to do is go in there and get it."

"What about the creepers?" Hunter asked. "How many?"

"Well, the good news is there aren't a thousand creepers in there," Gameknight said.

"A *thousand*?!" Hunter said.

"I said *not* a thousand . . . maybe only three hundred," he explained.

"You're happy with three hundred creepers in there, guarding the gunpowder?" Hunter asked.

"Better than a thousand," Gameknight replied with a smile.

"*Grrr*," growled Hunter.

"What we need is something to get the creepers out of their treasure room," Herder said.

"A diversion," Hunter said. "Exactly."

"But what?" Gameknight mused. "We don't have enough cats to scare them out."

"Do you have any redstone?" Hunter asked.

"Of course," Gameknight replied. "Crafter wouldn't let me leave the village without it." He handed over three stacks of the crimson dust.

"Then I know just what to do," she said with a smile. "Come on, Stitcher, we have a little surprise to build." She turned to Gameknight999. "Seal yourself into that chamber. I'll break it open when we're done."

Before he could respond, Hunter ran off with Stitcher following close behind.

"Herder," Gameknight said, gesturing to the lanky boy and then pointing to the sisters.

Herder nodded, then knelt by the wolves' pack leader.

"Go . . . protect," Herder said softly.

The animal gave a soft bark to the rest of the wolves, then took off running silently through the passage, following Hunter and Stitcher back up the tunnel. When they had disappeared around the curve, Gameknight sealed the doorway with blocks of dirt and waited. He placed a torch in the room so that they could see. The cats paced nervously about, some of them hissing at the dirt door that led to the treasure chamber. The animals could feel the creepers through the dirt and stone, and they wanted nothing more than to attack the mottled creatures.

After ten minutes, someone started knocking at the blocks that covered the entrance to the chamber. Quickly, Gameknight put out the torch and drew his swords. The magical enchantment on his weapon lit the chamber with a sparkling lavender hue. Herder moved to his side, his sword in hand, ready for a fight.

Just then, the top block shattered, and Stitcher's smiling face shone through the spray of dirt. She quickly dug up the second block, then squeezed into the room.

"Take off all your enchanted armor and put away your sword," Hunter said as she stepped into the room. She had a bow out, but it wasn't the normal enchanted bow that she liked so much. "We don't want the creepers to know we're here. If they see us, we're doomed, and they'll be coming by in about 3 . . . 2 . . . 1 . . ."

CHAPTER 21

THE TREASURE ROOM

A distant explosion rumbled through the stone and dirt, making the ground shake and dust fall from the ceiling.

Gameknight gave the sisters a questioning glance.

"Redstone timer circuit tied to some TNT," Stitcher said, a look of pride on her face.

The User-that-is-not-a-user smiled and nodded his head.

"Nice," he said.

"Get away from the doorway," Hunter said, then turned to face Herder. "Keep those animals quiet, especially the cats. Any sound and we'll be discovered. If you can't—"

Hunter paused as the shuffling of feet sounded outside the small room. Pressing her back to the wall, she stood next to the doorway, an arrow notched and ready. Gameknight moved beside her, holding a non-magical sword in his hand and wearing dull iron armor. He leaned forward so that he could see just the smallest sliver of the hallway, his body masked by the darkness of the stone chamber.

Creepers streamed out of the large gathering area, scurrying through the passage and heading toward the explosion. Just then, another detonation sounded, in a different location from the last one. Then another explosion rocked the hive . . . and another.

"It must be the User-that-is-not-a-user," said a voice from the hallway. "Find him and bring him before me . . . NOW!"

More creepers streaked past the opening, heading toward the explosions that continued to shake the hive, until everything eventually became completely quiet.

"You think it's safe now?" Gameknight asked.

"Wait," Herder said.

He knelt next to one of the cats and whispered in the tiger-striped animal's fuzzy ear. It glanced up at the skinny NPC, meowed softly, and then moved to the doorway. The creature disappeared for ten seconds, then returned and stared up at Herder. The cat seemed calm and relaxed.

"It's safe," Herder reported with a nod. "The creepers are gone."

Gameknight moved cautiously out into the passage and peeked down the tunnel; it was indeed empty. Walking quickly through the corridor, he entered the massive gathering chamber and found it also free of creepers. At the center of the room was that massive pile of gunpowder—in truth, made up of a whole bunch of smaller piles of the gray powder.

"Come on," Gameknight said.

He moved along the walls of the chamber, watching for any stray creepers in the shadows. Hunter and Stitcher did the same on the opposite walls. On one side, as they'd seen earlier, there was the lava flow spilling dangerously close to the pile of explosive dust. Gameknight pulled out a block of stone and used it to plug the flow of molten rock. The orange river of boiling stone slowly lowered to the ground, then disappeared, the pool of lava evaporating.

Suddenly, the cats started to hiss and growl. Gameknight spun around, his shimmering diamond sword suddenly in his hand.

"So, Gameknight999 returns," a hissing voice said from the other side of the chamber. "The User-that-is-not-a-user and Oxus, the king of the creepers, meet again. I warned you long ago that you would regret it if you ever showed your face in my kingdom. Now you must pay the penalty for your foolishness. You will never live to see the sky again."

Hunter and Stitcher pulled out their enchanted bows. The wooden bows creaked with strain as they both drew back an arrow and aimed toward the sound.

A purple flickering light shone out of a hidden alcove as a creeper moved into the open. It was the charged creeper Gameknight had seen earlier that sparkled with both a blue and red glow, as if it were somehow filled with redstone dust.

"You are not welcome here," the creeper king growled. "I told you before that if I saw you again, it would lead to your doom."

The monster glowed bright for just an instant, then dimmed as he regained control of his temper.

"What are you talking about?" Gameknight said, frowning. "I've never seen you before."

"You told me you would say that," the creeper king said. "Fine, we will play your game." He paused for a minute to let his glow subside. "I am Oxus, king of the creepers, and you are invading my kingdom."

"We are not here for a fight," Gameknight explained. "We just need some of your gunpowder so that we can save the Overworld from being destroyed."

"This gunpowder is our most sacred treasure," Oxus said. "Do you know how we get it?"

Gameknight shook his head.

"When a creeper is old and near death," Oxus explained, "they find the end of a tunnel. They then detonate themselves, expanding the hive with the last bit of their life. The gunpowder they drop after they explode is then brought here, so that we can remember their sacrifice. Each small pile represents the life of a single creeper. You may not touch it!"

"You don't have much to say about it," Hunter said as she drew her arrow back a little farther. "Here's the deal: if you stay where you are, we will let you live. But if you try to come closer, we will destroy you."

"You are all fools. I don't need to come closer. I am Oxus, king of the creepers. If I were to detonate right now, I would destroy all of you, regardless if you were near me or not. I could take out this entire room with the strength of my blast." Oxus glared at each of them. "This is my domain, and you are my prisoners. Lay down your arms and accept your punishment."

The creeper began to hiss and glow slightly. Hunter and Stitcher pointed their enchanted bows at him.

The king of the creepers laughed.

"You know nothing," Oxus said. "My ignition process will not stop just because you shoot me or hit me with your sword. The king of the creepers is different from normal creepers. I was made by Herobrine himself, and have capabilities you do not understand. My explosion will tear at your HP without hurting our precious treasure. Now put down your weapons or I will destroy you."

"Hunter, Stitcher . . . lower your bows," Gameknight said.

"What are you talking about?!" Hunter exclaimed.

"Just do it," he insisted.

They lowered their bows, causing Oxus to smile.

In one quick motion, Gameknight999 sprang into action, putting away his sword and immediately pulling out a torch. He then took three quick steps forward, holding the torch over the pile of gunpowder.

"I will destroy all of this gunpowder if you don't do what we say," Gameknight said.

"You wouldn't dare!" hissed Oxus.

"If we don't take some gunpowder with us, then all our friends will likely be destroyed," Gameknight said. "So we have nothing to lose."

The creeper king grew bright with anger, his rage causing him to begin the ignition process. Gameknight gasped when he saw how bright the monster had become—the creature's inner glow was like a mini sun. He breathed a sign of relief when the hissing finally diminished and the creeper king's body dimmed.

"Herder, bring your animals forward," the User-that-is-not-a-user said. "I want a ring of cats around the creeper king, and then a ring of wolves around them."

The lanky boy nodded his head, then knelt and spoke to the animals. Moving with lightning speed, the cats bolted across the floor and formed a circle around the glowing monster. Oxus tried to step back away from the felines but was quickly surrounded. He hissed at the animals, and they hissed back. The wolves then stood behind the cats, fur bristling and eyes glowing bright red; they were ready for battle.

"Stitcher, come fill your inventory," Gameknight said. "Hunter, keep an eye on the creeper king."

Hunter aimed her bow at the monster while Stitcher put away her bow and moved up to the massive gray pile. Quickly, she began scooping the individual piles of gunpowder into her inventory, forming stacks and stacks of the material.

"You can't take that!" Oxus roared. "You don't know what you are doing!"

"We have to take this so we can stop the blazes from destroying everything," Gameknight said. "If we don't stop them, they could ruin all of Minecraft."

"You don't understand!" Oxus shouted, his skin glowing bright. He then calmed himself and took a step forward. "Each small pile of gunpowder represents the life of a creeper—a friend and a family member. We come to the treasure room to remember our loved ones and honor those that died for the Hive. And now you are taking the last measure of their existence and using it in some foolish war."

Oxus started to become angry, glowing brighter and brighter. The cats began to hiss and move closer as the wolves growled. The creeper king glared down at the animals and calmed down.

"You gave me a message a long time ago," Oxus said as he glared at the User-that-is-not-a-user.

This caught Gameknight off-guard. *What is all this nonsense about us meeting,* he thought. *A trick?*

"What?" he asked.

"You gave me a message during the Great Zombie Invasion and told me to deliver it to you," the creeper king said. "You made me say it over and over until I had memorized it."

"What do you mean?" Gameknight asked. "How could I have talked to you during that war . . . ? It happened a hundred years ago."

"I don't know and I don't care," the king of the creepers replied. "I thought you were crazy at the time, but now I understand."

"What was the message?" Gameknight999 asked, confused.

"You said, 'Have faith in yourself, and don't worry what other people think. You must do what is right for those you care about, even if it means stepping aside for another to lead. Friends and family are more important, and sometimes the sword is not the answer.' A lot of that still makes no sense to me, but some I now understand."

Gameknight thought about the words. How could Oxus know what he was going through, that he was feeling unimportant and unappreciated? How could the king of the creepers know that he felt like an insignificant bug in Butch's shadow and that nobody listened to him? Was this message really from himself, from the past? *That's impossible,* he thought.

But then he thought hard about the words. The message focused on what was really important . . . friends and family. That's all he really cared about, making sure his friends and family were safe. It didn't matter if they really listened to Gameknight999 or not, or if he were viewed as their leader. As long as they were safe, nothing else mattered.

Gameknight glanced at the pile of gunpowder. This was of the creeper king's family, he realized, as it all sunk in. This was the last thing they ever saw of their loved ones, a reminder of their lives and how they gave the last of their lives to help expand the hive. It was truly a great treasure, and they couldn't misuse it.

"Stitcher, only take what we need," Gameknight said to the young girl.

"We should take it all," Hunter objected. "This much gunpowder can make a lot of TNT. We'd be set for a long time."

"No," the User-that-is-not-a-user said. "This is sacred to the creepers and we need to respect that. Three stacks should be sufficient . . . no more."

"But . . ."

"Hunter, all creatures deserve respect . . . even creepers," Gameknight said. "Sometimes the sword is not the answer." He turned and faced Oxus. "I'm sorry. I understand why you prize this gunpowder so much, and I respect that. But we need some, not only to save the lives of our friends, but also to save the Overworld. The blazes are trying to destroy everything and convert it to the Nether. Undoubtedly, they will want to cover most of the surface with lava after they destroy all the biomes. This will affect the creeper kingdom just as much as it will impact the NPCs. In this struggle, the NPCs and the creepers have a common enemy."

"The blazes, you say?" the creeper king said. "We have no love for blazes . . . not since the great war."

The glowing monster glanced down at Stitcher, who was taking gunpowder *out* of her inventory and putting back what they didn't need. He then glared at Hunter and sneered. Hunter sneered right back at him.

"Very well, you may have your three stacks," Oxus said. "But let me be clear about something." He took a step closer to Gameknight999. The cats hissed and the wolves growled, but the creeper king ignored the animals and stared at the User-that-is-not-a-user. "You are not welcome in the creeper Hive. If you return again, you will be destroyed. If we find you on the surface, we will try to destroy you. What the creepers of my kingdom want most is to be left alone, and your intrusions are not appreciated."

Gameknight nodded his head with understanding.

"Just as I told you a hundred years ago, we will part ways without violence . . . for now, but do not cross my path again. Do you understand?"

Gameknight nodded again, even though he still didn't get the part about meeting the creeper king one hundred years ago.

"I cannot guarantee your safety when you leave here," the king of the creepers said. "But there is a hidden passage behind me. It will take you through my personal chambers and to the surface. If you are fast, and lucky, you may live to see the sky again. Now go, before I lose my patience and change my mind about letting you live."

"Thank you, Oxus," Gameknight said. "We will not return to your kingdom. Its location will remain a secret and will not be disclosed to anyone. On this, you have my word."

"Just go," Oxus snapped. "Your presence here offends me."

"I understand," Gameknight said. He withdrew the torch and put it back into his inventory, then turned to the sisters. "Hunter, put down your bow. It's time to go. Herder, gather your animals. I'm sure Oxus would appreciate it if you had the cats back off some."

Herder nodded and whistled once. The cats and wolves came flocking to him and formed a protective ring around the NPC. Stitcher then stood and moved next to the clowder of cats. Gameknight stepped to Hunter's side and put a hand on the arrow she had notched and aimed, pushing it downward and away from the creeper. Oxus looked at him, gave a wry smile, and then moved to the side. Behind the creeper king was a dark passage that sloped upward before disappearing into the darkness.

Gameknight grabbed Hunter by the sleeve and pulled her into the entranceway, then gave her a gentle shove up the ascending tunnel. Stitcher followed, along with Herder and his animals, leaving Gameknight999 alone with the king of the creepers.

"One more thing, Gameknight999," Oxus said when they were alone.

"What?"

"I know who you are, and your secret remains safe with me," the creeper king said. "But if you ever return to my kingdom, I will tell all the NPCs, and it will shatter their faith in their history as well as their faith in you. The NPCs will never trust you again."

"I have no idea what you're talking about," Gameknight replied, confused.

"I won't play your game, User-that-is-not-a-user," Oxus said with a hiss, his body glowing bright. "Consider this a final warning. Now get out of my kingdom."

Gameknight stared at the creeper king, confused and about to ask another question, when he heard the sound of shuffling feet growing louder. The creepers were returning. Turning, the User-that-is-not-a-user charged into the darkness of the tunnel after his friends, leaving the angry king of the creepers alone with hatred in his malevolent eyes.

CHAPTER 22

RISING FROM LAVA

The two NPCs finished piling Nether quartz blocks into the shape of a tall rectangle near the Great Lava Ocean. The interior of the rectangle was open, with nothing to support the top blocks other than the two vertical sides. The opening was two blocks wide by three blocks tall, easily large enough to allow creatures to pass through. Peering up at the blaze king, the two prisoners backed away from the ring and lowered their heads to the ground.

Charybdis laughed, his internal flame flickering with each chuckle.

"You NPCs are so pathetic," he wheezed. "Like obedient little pets, you accept the leash and welcome your cage as if you were meant to be oppressed."

The NPCs said nothing, knowing resistance was futile. A shovel, pickaxe, food, and torches floated off the ground near the newly-constructed rectangle: the remains of the last villager to object to the blaze king's commands.

Floating to the lava ocean, Charybdis sunk down so that his blaze rods were just barely brushing the surface of the molten stone. A strange, sickly yellow glow flowed up from the lava and stained the king's internal flame, changing it from bright orange to something that appeared sallow and diseased. With an intense burst of power, the blaze launched a fireball at the Nether quartz ring. The white-hot fireball hit the open rectangle and exploded into an orange sheet that sparkled and undulated within the stone rectangle as if it were alive.

"Scouts, see where this leads," the blaze king commanded.

Two blazes moved quickly forward and passed through the orange sheet of fire. Instantly, they disappeared, vanishing from the Nether. In seconds, they returned back through the portal and stared up at their king.

"A snow-covered forest," one of the monsters said.

"Perfect," Charybdis said. "Something about the burning of trees and melting of snow into steam just makes me happy." He glanced down at his warriors, their dark eyes staring up at him expectantly. "Burn it . . . a dozen of you should be able to level that forest to the ground. Then scorch the soil into glass."

The blazes grew bright with excitement, then floated through the portal. In minutes, dark smoke trickled out of the orange sheet, carrying with it the faint scent of burning pine.

Charybdis laughed.

Just then, the blaze general floated up out of the lava ocean, the molten stone oozing off his circulating blaze rods like thick honey. Behind him, hundreds of smaller blazes emerged, each with a flame half as bright as the generals, their glowing blaze rods spinning with intense effort.

"Ahh . . . my new blazes have hatched I see," Charybdis said. "Well done, General—you make an excellent egg-tender."

The blazes that floated along the shoreline chuckled, the fire connecting their blaze rods flickering with laughter.

"Lead the blazelings to the shoreline and let them feed," the blaze king said. "We need these young ones to be strong and eager."

The general glided to the shoreline as he glared at the other blazes, many of them still laughing. He looked up at his king and gave him the best smile he could manage, seeing that he was being humiliated. Reaching the shoreline, the general moved out of the lava and across the netherrack ground until he floated next to his king.

"You have done well, commander," Charybdis said. "Consider your punishment complete. Perhaps next time you will not let a village survive when I order it destroyed."

"Yes, Sire," the general said, obediently.

"Come, my children, feed on the fires of the Great Lava Ocean," Charybdis said to the newborns. "Let the heat of Minecraft and the magical powers of Herobrine make you strong, for the lava in which you were born is imbued with the Maker's powers."

The small blazelings moved out of the lava ocean, the glowing liquid stone dripping off them and splattering onto the ground. They moved along the shoreline, then dipped their blaze rods into the lava and drank in the nourishing heat. Each began to glow brighter as their internal flames grew bigger and hotter. Lava dripped upward from the ocean, landed on their rotating blaze rods, and made them grow longer and longer—the young monsters became taller and stronger and hotter right before Charybdis' eyes. He chuckled gleefully as he watched, his wheezing breath sounding like a robotic machine of terror.

The blaze king then tore his dark eyes from the blaze hatchings and turned to the NPC prisoners.

"I want more Nether quartz portals built . . . NOW!" he commanded. "Fifteen of them . . . and make it fast, before I lose my patience."

The slaves did not even bother to complain. They just picked up their pickaxes and shuffled forward. From the chest that sat nearby, each took out rusty blocks of Nether quartz ore, the white crystalline quartz shining brightly through the center of the cube. One of the villagers dug two holes in the ground and then filled them with Nether quartz. Two others started placing the blocks on top of each other, next to the two embedded cubes, forming a stack of four. A third villager placed blocks of netherrack beneath his feet as he jumped into the air. When he was high enough, he placed the cubes across the top, enclosing the rectangle.

Quickly, the villagers scurried from the empty portal. They knew Charybdis would not wait for the NPCs to be safely away before lighting the magical doorway. Sure enough, a fireball from the monster hit the portal almost immediately after they were out of the way, the flaming explosion creating a thin sheet of flame across the Nether quartz ring.

"Hurry, I want more," Charybdis wheezed. "You are all pathetic and too slow. I should destroy all of you just for making me wait. Or maybe I'll just throw one of you into the lava ocean to motivate the rest."

Instantly, the villagers began working harder, running from place to place so as to escape the blaze king's scrutiny. Just for fun, Charybdis threw some fireballs near the NPCs. Two of them screamed out in fear, which made the king of the blazes laugh.

"You see, General, that's how you handle these villagers," Charybdis said. "You need to be firm with them and let them know who is boss. Never let them believe that defiance is an option, unless they no longer wish to live."

The general nodded his head as Charybdis lit the next portal with his scorching white-hot balls of fire.

"Watch over these idiotic villagers while I gather the rest of our forces," the blaze king said.

He floated away from the shoreline and unfinished portals and moved to a rectangular pen made of netherrack. Within the enclosure was his blaze-horse, a gift from Herobrine. The animal had been crafted at the same time that Charybdis himself had been created, and it had proven useful for moving across the Nether quickly.

Gathering a ball of fire, he launched it at the side of the enclosure, blasting open one wall. The blaze horse, made just of blaze rods and fire, reminded Charybdis of a skeleton horse. The creature had no skin, no tissue or muscles. It was composed only of the glowing blaze rods, like the blaze king himself. But the horse's blaze rods did not spin about like they did for Charybdis. Rather, they were fused together, serving as the creature's skeleton, a wreath of flame surrounding each.

The blaze-horse came to Charybdis' side, instantly eager to please its master. The king of the blazes floated to the top of the creature and then settled atop its back. Once he was seated, his circulating blaze rods finally stopped.

"We must find all our brothers, my friend," Charybdis said to the large creature. "Let's ride across the Nether and bring them all here."

The horse whinnied, causing plumes of flame to shoot out of its glowing nostrils, then bolted forward, streaking across the landscape. Nudging the creature with his motionless blaze rods, Charybdis guided the horse through the smoky landscape. He didn't bother to avoid the many lava streams and pools, as they were as mother's milk to the flaming beast. They splashed through the liquid stone, the heat from the fiery rivers nourishing horse and rider alike.

As they rode, the blaze king called out to his subjects, commanding them to go to the Nether fortress. He knew they would need every monster they could assemble to finish the destruction of the Overworld, and at the same time, attack Gameknight999. Charybdis would not make the same mistake the other monster kings had: underestimating the User-that-is-not-the-user. He wanted overwhelming forces with him when he faced his nemesis to ensure total victory.

Streaking across the Nether, the blaze king saw the word spreading. Blazes were flowing toward the citadel in droves, although the foolish zombie-pigmen continued their random walks across the burning landscape. *The zombies barely have enough intelligence to form single words*, the blaze king thought with a huff. Since the loss of Herobrine, the pigmen had been difficult, if not impossible, to control. They were useless to Charybdis.

Spinning his flaming mount around, he headed back toward his Nether fortress. As he rode down a steep sloping hill, Charybdis could see the glowing forms of his subjects that had already arrived, waiting for their king around the still-unfinished portals. Very soon, he would have his massive army and would be ready for his assault against Gameknight999. But first, he had to make the Overworld suffer.

Heading for the stone pen, the blaze king guided the horse to its enclosure, then leapt off when he was safely inside.

"You did well, my steed," Charybdis said to his blaze-horse.

The creature whinnied, then moved to the small pool of lava and drank heartily.

Causing his blaze rods to spin again, the king floated up into the air and moved across the smoky plain to his now-finished Nether quartz doorways. Drawing on his internal flame, he threw super-heated balls of fire at the portals, lighting them until a flickering sheet of fire was contained within each. Fifteen portals now glowed before him, each one linked to a different part of the Overworld.

"I want a dozen blazes to go through each portal and destroy everything," Charybdis said. "The NPCs will not know which way to look or where we will hit next. This distraction will give us time to assemble the rest of our forces."

He gazed down at his warriors. They all burned brightly with excitement and confidence, which pleased him immensely.

"Once the area is destroyed, come back through the portal. This attack will draw the User-that-is-not-a-user to us, and we must be prepared for his arrival. We will surprise him with our massive army and crush him on the shores of the Great Lava Ocean. Now GO!"

The eager blazes flared brightly as they whooshed through the portals. Charybdis wheezed and cackled with glee as smoke and ash began to stream back through the shimmering orange sheets and into the Nether—evidence of the destruction happening all across the Overworld.

CHAPTER 23

GATEWAY OF FIRE

They made it out of the creeper hive . . . but just barely. As they ran through the escape tunnel Oxus had showed them, the party was surprised by a group of three creepers.

Not giving them a chance to react, Gameknight charged at the trio and attacked. Using his two swords, the User-that-is-not-a-user slashed at whichever creeper was trying to ignite, halting each one's detonation process until all three monsters were destroyed. Unfortunately, they didn't see that there was a fourth one hiding in the shadows.

"There's one more!" Stitcher yelled as the creature hissed. "*Run!*"

They ran up the ascending passage, a wave of fur streaking past the four companions. And then the monster exploded. The blast and heat shot up the tunnel toward them, and the walls began to shake. The four companions leapt forward and fell to the ground, just escaping the blast radius.

A cloud of dust billowed around them. Gameknight coughed and sat up.

"Everyone okay?" he asked.

"Yeah . . . that was close, though," Stitcher said, dusting herself off. "A little *too* close, don't you think?"

"Hey, where are the animals?" Herder asked.

A bark sounded from farther up the ascending tunnel. Drawing a torch from his inventory, Gameknight held it out in front of him. The circle of light pushed back the darkness, revealing the four of them; they were each covered in dust and dirt, and they were alone. No animals were near.

"Where are my friends?" Herder said in a low voice.

A tiny square tear tumbled down the boy's face, clearing the dust and leaving clean traces on his square cheeks.

"I'm sure they're OK," Stitcher said.

"Maybe they didn't make it out," Hunter said.

"No, I hear something up ahead," the User-that-is-not-a-user said.

With the torch held out before him, Gameknight walked slowly up the rising passage. Suddenly, spots of light appeared in the darkness; golden eyes were staring at the four friends out of the darkness.

"What's that?" Hunter asked as she notched an arrow and pulled it back.

Herder reached out and pushed her arrow downward, then walked forward, a huge smile on his face. Out of the darkness came his "friends," the cats and wolves having streaked through the passage just before the blast.

"Are they OK?" Stitcher asked as the rest of the party walked forward and stood next to the young boy.

Herder glanced about the passage and counted the animals, then sighed. Turning he gave his companions a huge smile.

"They're all here," he said.

Gameknight realized he had been holding his breath, and he gulped in some air as tension left his body.

"I'll be back," he said.

The User-that-is-not-a-user then ran down the passageway to inspect the damage. When he reached the explosion site, he could see the tunnel was completely blocked; piles of sand and gravel filled the space, blocking the creepers from reaching them. Turning, he returned to his friends.

"The passage is blocked," Gameknight reported. "No creepers will sneak up behind us . . . for now."

"Then let's get out of here," Hunter said.

The group ran around the base of the volcano until they found their horses. Fortunately, the animals were still tied to the fence post Herder had placed in the ground. Not waiting for discussion or plans, the four friends jumped into the saddle and rode as fast as they could from the flaming mountain and the furious monsters that dwelled under the smoking peak.

All of them knew they had to get back to Crafter's village as soon as possible. With the three stacks of gunpowder, they could make almost two hundred splash potions of fire resistance; that would easily be enough to protect the NPCs against the fireballs of the blazes.

But it would only be useful if they made it back in time.

Pushing their horses hard, the companions traveled as fast as they could, the cats and wolves easily keeping pace. After an hour, though, the horses began to show some fatigue.

"We need to slow down," Gameknight said as he pulled back on the reins and shifted to a trot.

His horse whinnied her appreciation.

The others did the same, slowing to match Gameknight's pace. They shifted from trotting to running to sprinting through the rest of the night and into the morning. When the sun rose in front of them, they were well through the desert, the tall watchtower of the desert village just barely visible off to the right. Ahead, Gameknight could see the tall spruces of the taiga, the leafy foliage frosted with a layer of snow. The biome seemed rich with life compared with the sparse desert. The trees reached high up into the air, as if trying to touch the sun.

Suddenly, a column of smoke began to rise into the air.

"Fire!" Gameknight shouted.

He kicked his horse into a gallop and charged forward. As he rode, he pulled out his enchanted bow and notched an arrow. Glancing over his shoulder, he could see the sisters had done the same.

Charging across the desert, Gameknight passed into the cold taiga after a five-minute sprint. The cold air shocked him, as he'd become accustomed to the dry, harsh environment. Now, the world was cool, with snow covering the trees and ground. The horses' hooves made a curious crunching sound as they pierced the frozen layer.

Gameknight followed the smoke through the trees. Glowing balls of fire were streaking down from overhead, exploding when they hit trees and the ground. The blazes were attacking the forest.

The fastest way to the village was straight through the forest; they couldn't afford to go the long way. They'd have to fight. He motioned for everyone to stop, and then came to a halt, circling back around to face his friend so that he could speak in a low voice and still be heard by the others.

"Stay on your horse and keep moving," Gameknight said. "Use your bows. Fire, then move, then fire again. If we stand still, we're done for. Everyone understand?"

The three NPCs nodded their heads.

Gameknight could see that even Herder held a bow. Hunter or Stitcher had probably given it to him. It wasn't likely he'd hit anything, but Gameknight thought it was good that he was there to add his arrows to their attack.

Gameknight kicked his horse into a gallop and charged toward the glowing shapes in the sky. As he neared, he fired two quick shots at the closest airborne blaze. But he'd been too slow, for Hunter's and Stitcher's arrows had already hit it. Instantly, the creature flared bright and then disappeared as its blaze rods clattered to the ground.

Turning quickly to the right, he found another target and charged. As he approached, Gameknight saw something glowing bright orange near the ground. Figuring it was another blaze, he drew his diamond sword and readied his attack. But when he was near, he realized it was another of those strange fiery portals he'd seen earlier. But this one was hundreds of blocks from the last one.

How can this be? Gameknight thought.

And then it hit him: the blazes could put a portal anywhere they wanted to.

"Oh no," the User-that-is-not-a-user said.

"What's wrong?" Hunter asked as she pulled up alongside her friend.

"This is another blaze portal," Gameknight explained. "It means they can place them anywhere they want in the Overworld. How can we stop an enemy that can appear anywhere . . . everywhere . . . at a moment's notice?"

"That means they might appear at our village any second!" Hunter exclaimed.

"Finally, the pathetic NPCs understand that their destruction is near," boomed a voice from overhead, interrupting them.

Gameknight and Hunter both looked up to see a vicious blaze staring down at them. Hunter started to raise her bow, but another voice from behind stopped her.

"I wouldn't do that," another monster wheezed.

Gameknight glanced over his shoulder and saw two more blazes behind them. Then two more closed in on either side, completely surrounding them.

"Stitcher and Herder are still out there," Hunter whispered. "When they fire, we'll—"

"Your friends cannot help you," the blaze said, having overheard their conversation. "We have them trapped as well. You will be four new prizes for the king of the blazes. His current slaves are becoming too weak to be of much use anymore. I will bring him four new slaves, and he will be very pleased indeed. Now keep your weapons down, or the other blazes will be forced to fire upon you."

Gameknight and Hunter both lowered their bows to their sides and glared up at the monsters. Glancing around, the User-that-is-not-a-user knew he had to find a way out. He needed to get the information about the blaze portals to Crafter and his friends, but they were caught. There was no way to escape without being bombarded with fireballs.

He glanced at Hunter and smiled.

"Fighting is better than surrendering, right?" Gameknight whispered.

"I've been in a cage before," Hunter said. "I won't go back again, not while I can still draw breath."

"But if we try to escape, they're sure to open fire on us," Gameknight said. "I doubt we stand much of a chance."

"Trying is better than quitting," Hunter replied in a low voice.

"Ok, then," he replied.

Fear pulsed through his veins as he thought about what would happen next, but he knew he had to try. After all, quitting wasn't his thing. Gripping his bow tightly in his head, Gameknight999 steeled himself for the fiery attack about to rain down on them both.

CHAPTER 24

AN UNEXPECTED FRIEND

Suddenly, snowballs flew up from the ground and smashed into one of the blazes. The icy spheres made the creature's internal flame sputter and flicker and then, with additional hits, go out completely. The monster's face took on a look of surprise, then terror, as its blaze rods fell apart and tumbled to the ground.

With the other blazes shocked at the turn of events, Gameknight and Stitcher kicked their mounts into a gallop. They both brought up their bows and fired, and were instantly joined by more arrows streaking out of a nearby smoky cloud. Gameknight fired three quick shots at one blaze, while Hunter took out another. He knew the other flaming arrows were Stitcher's and the normal arrows were Herders, but who was responsible for the snowballs?

A blaze popped out directly in front of them, emerging from behind a burning tree. The User-that-is-not-a-user pulled back on the reins, causing his horse to rear up on her back legs. It made it impossible for him to shoot, so instead, he veered to the left, giving Hunter a clear shot. The blaze flared bright, ready to fire down upon Gameknight999, but it never had a chance. Hunter's pointed barbs took its HP to zero in the blink of an eye. The creature disappeared with a pop, leaving behind three glowing sticks and balls of XP.

Turning in a tight circle, Gameknight spotted another group of monsters. As he rode, he could see more snowballs streaking up into the air, hitting one monster, then the next and the next. But where were they coming from? By the time he'd reached the group of blazes, only one monster remained. Drawing an arrow, Gameknight fired at the same time as Hunter did behind him. Their arrows hit the creature simultaneously. With its HP almost to zero, it started to sink to the ground, too weak to stay aloft.

Gameknight turned away from the wounded monster and sought out other targets. They were easy to see in the smoke, their bright flames creating orange halos that shone bright through the ash.

"Hunter, are you behind me?" he asked.

"Sure am," she replied.

"Take the one on the left, up ahead; I'll get the one on the right," Gameknight said.

She grunted her understanding.

They charged ahead, riding for the space between the two blazes. Once they were within bowshot, Gameknight skidded to a stop, then drew an arrow and aimed. He fired, then drew and fired again, then drew and fired a third arrow. His first shot struck the monster when the third one left the bow, but he could see the second shot had missed.

Before he could draw a fourth and final blow, an arrow streaked through the hazy air from the side and struck the monster, extinguishing its flame and causing the monster to disappear. Scanning the air, he searched for any other blazes, but the only thing glowing through the billowing clouds was the burning trees.

Kicking his horse back into a gallop, Gameknight headed for the portal. He had to swerve around burning spruces and falling trees, but he finally reached the glowing rectangle. He dismounted and approached it carefully. It looked like a thin sheet of fire that undulated and pulsed, as if it had a heart beat.

Hoof beats caused the User-that-is-not-a-user to turn. With an arrow drawn, he stared into the smoke, waiting to see if it was friend or foe, only to spot Hunter emerging, her own arrow pointed at him. He smiled as they both lowered their weapons, then he turned back to the portal. Heat seemed to pour from the rectangle, making Gameknight afraid to get too much closer.

"Hmmm . . . be careful," said a voice from the smoke that he didn't recognize. "That portal will suck the HP right from your body."

Gameknight jumped, startled, and turned toward the direction of the voice. Stitcher and Herder then came walking out of the smoke with another NPC, clad in all white. As they neared, Gameknight could see that it wasn't an NPC—it was a light-crafter!

Gameknight knew some of the light-crafters, like Treebrin and Grassbrin, who lived in Crafter's village. Plus, he'd met Woodbrin before storming the Source long ago. And recently he'd had the help of Icebrin in defeating Herobrine in dragon form. But this light-crafter before Gameknight999 was someone new.

Putting away his bow, Gameknight stepped forward to greet the stranger, but before he could speak, the light-crafter pulled out balls of snow and fired them at the portal. The icy spheres hit the flaming sheet and made it flicker once, then again, and then finally extinguished it, closing the gateway between the Overworld and the Nether.

"Who are you?" Gameknight asked.

"I am Snowbrin," the light-crafter said.

"He saved us!" Stitcher said. "Herder and I were surrounded, but he destroyed three of the blazes before they even knew what was happening."

"We are grateful for your help," Gameknight999 said. "But how did you—"

"Let's save the introductions. Right now, I think we should get out of the forest," Hunter said, her eyes still scanning the sky for monsters.

"You're right," the User-that-is-not-a-user said.

Walking to his horse, he swung up into the saddle, then let Herder jump up behind him.

"Where are your horses?" Hunter asked.

Gameknight felt his friend stiffen at the question.

"The blazes shot them out from under us," Stitcher said. "They did not suffer, though. Those fireballs were much hotter than we expected. The animals didn't stand a chance."

"Come on, let's go," Hunter said. "We can have a nice little chat when we're safe."

"Hunter is right. Let's get out of here," Gameknight said. "Snowbrin, do you need—"

"Hmmm . . . don't worry about me," the light-crafter said. "I have work to do here still. You continue on your journey, and I will catch up."

"But we're on horseback," Stitcher said. "How will you keep up?"

"You'll understand when I see you again," Snowbrin said.

And then Snowbrin turned and ran toward the flames, throwing clumps of snowballs that landed on the ground and merged into blocks of snow. With the intense heat of the fire, the blocks instantly melted and turned to water, extinguishing the flames nearby. Glancing over his shoulder, he flashed Gameknight a grin and then disappeared into the smoke.

"Come on, we need to get back to Crafter and the village," Gameknight said. "The blaze king can apparently make a portal anywhere he wants. They could be making one right now that would drop them right in the middle of the village, catching everyone by surprise. We have to get back and warn them."

Kicking the horse into a gallop, Gameknight shot out of the burning forest with Hunter right behind. As they rode, they could hear the splashes of water behind them, as Snowbrin's blocks melted and slowly extinguished the forest fire. The forest was badly damaged but not destroyed. This biome could still support life, and that felt like a victory against the blazes—the first one in a long time.

Turning to the east, they continued their journey toward home, the burning forest slowly receding behind them. But as they rode, Gameknight had a feeling they were going to be too late, and that something really, *really* bad was happening at that moment to his friends.

We've got the gunpowder, so all that's left to do is follow Butch's lead, Gameknight thought. *Maybe we should go to the Nether and attack.*

Still, there was something about Butch's plan that made Gameknight hesitate. The heat of those fireballs was terrifying. He wasn't one-hundred-percent sure a potion of fire resistance would last long against those super-heated spheres of death. They needed something to give them an advantage, and Gameknight999 could feel that splash potions, while extremely useful, might not be enough on their own to ensure victory.

Just then, a scratching, scraping sound reached their ears from behind them. Glancing over his shoulder, the User-that-is-not-a-user saw a blurry figure streaking toward them, leaving a long trail of white behind it. He quickly realized that it was Snowbrin, and to Gameknight's surprise, the light-crafter was streaking along on a path of snow that he was creating directly in front of his feet, moving like a speed skater with magical skates. This must be part of Snowbrin's light-crafting magic, Gameknight realized: the ability to create snow at will and dash across it like a frosty bullet. That was how he had defeated the blazes and extinguished the forest fire.

Instantly, images began to pop into the User-that-is-not-a-user's head, and the puzzle pieces began to tumble again.

"Blocks of snow . . . of course," Gameknight said to himself.

"What did you say?" Stitcher asked.

But he was lost in the puzzle, lost in the plan and searching for the solution that would save all his friends and Minecraft.

"We'll need lots of—" Gameknight said, but was interrupted by Herder.

"I know what you're thinking," Herder said from behind. "There is a large patch in the village . . . and they're ripe."

"Ahh . . . what?" Gameknight asked.

But before Herder could answer, Snowbrin was sliding along at their side.

"Hmmm . . . we must hurry," the light-crafter said. "The blazes are becoming bolder in their attacks. They must be stopped."

"I have an idea, but we'll need your help," Gameknight said.

"What do you have in mind?" Hunter asked.

"Something that Stitcher is going to hate," Gameknight said with a smile.

"In that case, I like it!" the older sister replied.

The User-that-is-not-a-user smiled at the girls, then kicked his horse into a sprint and charged toward their village and their friends.

CHAPTER 25

THE CAT WAITS FOR THE MOUSE

Charybdis stared in shock at the dark rectangle of Nether quartz.

The blazes had all been able to go through the other portals, destroy their targets, and return, but something went wrong this time.

The blazes entered the portal. Smoke began to stream out of the fiery gateway, like before, showing the blaze king that the forest was aflame. But then a metallic clanking noise came through the portal. It sounded like a blacksmith banging away on an anvil with a big hammer. The clanking sounded again and again, and all the monsters knew what it meant: the blazes in that forest were taking damage. Then came the last agonizing groans of all the flaming monsters being destroyed. One after the next, the creatures were fading away as the unknown attackers continued their assault.

Charybdis wanted to send more blazes immediately, but he'd already sent most of his troops through the other portals, and he didn't want to use up all his reserve forces with this battle. That would have left the Nether fortress unprotected. When some of the blazes returned from the other portals, Charybdis readied a counter-attack; but suddenly, just as he was about to order a second wave of flaming soldiers through, the portal winked out. The delicate sheet of flame that pulsed within the Nether quartz ring just seemed to vanish, as if it had been extinguished from the other side.

"How dare they harm my blazes and destroy my portal!" the blaze king screamed as his internal flame grew bright. He could only think of one person that could disrupt his plans so completely: the User-that-is-not-a-user.

"I have a feeling we will have a visitor soon, my friends," Charybdis said to the blazes around him. "We must prepare an appropriate welcome for him."

When the rest of his warriors had finished their destructive tasks and returned through the other still-working fiery portals, the king motioned for one of the NPCs to break the Nether quartz rings. Using a pickaxe, the villager broke away one block from each ring, instantly extinguishing the flickering gateway.

Staring across the Nether, Charybdis could see more blazes floating toward the fortress. He'd ridden far across the burning landscape, calling his people to him, and they had answered his call. Likely, there were a hundred monsters floating across the netherrack, heading for his mighty citadel. With the new blazelings and his existing arsenal of warriors, he still probably had over two hundred monsters at his disposal, even with the loss of the blazes that had just been destroyed in the forest fight.

Spinning his blaze rods quickly, the king of the blazes rose into the air and gazed down upon his army. They all stared up at him with expectant, fiery eyes.

"My children, a great day will soon be upon us," Charybdis shrieked, his voice echoing across the Nether. "We will soon destroy our ancient enemy, the User-that-is-not-a-user."

The flames of the blazes flickered with excitement.

"But we must prepare a little surprise, for I suspect he will be coming to pay us a little visit. We will allow him to come to the Nether, and we will even allow him to come to our fortress."

Many of the blazes appeared confused, their internal flames dimming a bit.

"But have no fear . . . we will be ready for Gameknight999 and his NPC friends," Charybdis announced. "We will let them come near, but then some of you will attack out of the Nether fortress, while the rest of the army ambushes them from hidden caves. We will surround them before they even know what's happening. And when they think the trap is complete, I will have another surprise ready for them, just for fun. These NPCs will know they have come to meet their doom. Then we will take our time exterminating them, saving the User-that-is-not-a-user for last."

The blazes began to laugh, their flames growing bright.

"General, have your lieutenants use their fireballs to carve out deep caves in the netherrack," Charybdis commanded. "Make them deep and curving, so that our blazes can hide and await our enemy's arrival. Use those two hills over there." The blaze king launched a pair of fireballs at some distant hills, marking their location. "Understood?"

"Yes, Sire," the general replied.

He then floated higher and let his internal flame grow white-hot. The orange glow from the lava ocean was pushed aside by his blazing white light, making it almost appear like it was daytime in the subterranean world.

"We will do what none of the other monsters in Minecraft have been able to do," Charybdis screamed. "WE WILL DESTROY GAMEKNIGHT999!"

The blazes wheezed and flickered as they shot their fireballs straight up into the air, creating a beautiful and lethal fireworks show.

Slowly, Charybdis floated back to the ground as the blazes moved off, all preparing for the battle to come. The blaze king watched his subjects prepare, and a feeling of glee filled him from head to blaze rod.

"Soon, Gameknight999, you will be kneeling before me, begging for mercy. But you will receive none!"

CHAPTER 26

OLD FRIENDS

Gameknight smiled when he saw the bright torches that trimmed the top of the fortified wall; they'd made it home. The village seemed lonely now that there was no forest surrounding the grassy plain. Much of the ash and soot that covered the ghostly remains of the trees and plants had been blown away by the wind. Without the black, dusty covering, the devastated landscape seemed like something on an alien planet. It reminded Gameknight of a Minecraft mod he'd once played, called Galacticraft.

"This just makes me sad," Stitcher said as she glared at the forest. "Will it always be this way?"

"What do you mean?" Gameknight asked.

"I mean, will the trees ever grow back again?"

Gameknight shrugged, then turned and stared at Snowbrin. The light-crafter was gliding along next to him on a layer of snow blocks as if he were ice-skating. The blocks of pristine white powder formed in front of him just before he would take his next step. Behind him, the path trailed off and slowly melted as the sun beat down on the frozen cubes.

"What do you think, Snowbrin?" Gameknight asked.

"Hmmm," Snowbrin said.

Gameknight noticed the light-crafter seemed to make this sound whenever lost in thought.

"I have been in Minecraft for a long time," Snowbrin said. "Since the great war . . . the pre-alpha days, as they were called. Hmmm . . . I have seen a lot of things, some wonderful and some terrible, but there is one thing that always seems to stay constant."

"What?" Hunter asked. "That you always take a long time to answer a question?"

Stitcher punched her sister in the arm.

"Ouch," she complained.

Stitcher smiled.

"Hmmm . . . though you are correct, Hunter, that is not my observation," Snowbrin said. "What I have learned is that Minecraft always seems to find a way to bring life into existence. After the great war, many were killed, but life continued. Sections of the world were destroyed and shattered by explosions and fire, yet life found a way to return. So, I do not think this damage is permanent, as long as the blazes are stopped. If left unchecked, I fear the blazes may succeed in destroying the Overworld and throwing Minecraft forever out of balance, and that is much more serious."

"Why is being out of balance such a big deal?" Gameknight asked.

"Because if it gets too far out of balance, then it could threaten the stability of the Source," Snowbrin said. "That would cause all the servers to shut down. Minecraft could not recover from that. All the lives on all the server planes would be extinguished in the blink of an eye. We cannot allow that to happen."

"Oh, no," Gameknight said.

"That's all you have to say? 'Oh, no'?" Hunter said.

"Not that . . . look!" the User-that-is-not-a-user said, pointing to the tall cobblestone walls.

They all turned and looked toward the village.

"What are you worried about?" Hunter said. "I don't see anything."

"Exactly," he replied.

"Wait, where is everyone?" Herder asked.

"I don't know," Gameknight replied, "but I think we'd better hurry up."

He kicked his horse into a sprint, crossed the last bit of the bare forest, and passed into the thick grass of the plain. As he rode, Gameknight scanned the battlements and archer towers, searching for any guards on duty. There were none, as far as he could tell.

Slowing to a gallop, then to a canter, Gameknight crossed the wooden bridge that spanned the moat, dismounted, and approached the village gates. Drawing his diamond sword in his right hand and his iron in his left, he motioned for Herder to open the doors.

Once they were open just enough to squeeze through, he charged inside, with Hunter and Stitcher right on his heels. They quickly spread throughout the village, scanning the area for threats. Herder pulled the horses through the doors, then released the reins as he followed Gameknight, with Snowbrin at his side.

The User-that-is-not-a-user raced up the steps that led to the top of the wall and glanced around. There was no one atop the tall watchtower . . . not a good sign. Animal pens sat empty, as did horse corrals. The village was completely deserted: no monsters, no villagers, no animals . . . nothing.

"Where do you think they went?" Herder asked.

"I don't know," Gameknight replied. "Send out your animals and have them scout the village and my castle. They can use the tunnel that connects the two."

Herder nodded, then moved down the steps to his friends. Crouching, he spoke softly to the wolves and cats and then whistled. Instantly, the animals shot away like a furry explosion. The wolves searched the village, while the cats took the tunnel that led to Gameknight's castle.

Moving down the steps, the User-that-is-not-a-user stood next to the lanky boy's side and paced back and forth, nervous of what the animals might find—or might *not* find.

"There must be someone here," Gameknight mumbled to himself. "We have to learn what happened. If we don't, then—"

Suddenly, a black cat streaked from the tunnel that led to the castle like a bolt of shadowy lightning, heading straight for Herder. When the animal drew near, it started to yowl as if it were in distress. Reaching down, Herder stroked its back, then glanced up at Gameknight999.

"They're in your castle," the young boy reported.

"Come on," Gameknight said as he took off running.

Behind him, the User-that-is-not-a-user could hear Herder whistling for the other animals. As he ran, his friend's footsteps pounded on the dirt and gravel behind him, following closely on his heels. They streaked through the underground passageway that ran between the village and the castle and emerged within the obsidian walls of Castle Gameknight.

Turning, the User-that-is-not-a-user was about to run through the doors of the keep when one of them flung open and Morgana, the village witch, emerged.

"It's about time you showed up," she said with a scratchy voice. "They left a few hours ago, but I'm sure that fool, Butch, already has everyone in hot water."

"Morgana, what are you talking about?" Gameknight asked.

"Butch, the idiot . . . he convinced all of them to go with him to the Nether," she said. "Everyone that could carry a sword agreed. He slowly got them all worked up, and when the warriors from the other villages arrived, that was all they needed to convince themselves to go after the blazes right away. They used some of your obsidian and built a portal upstairs, and then they went through."

Gameknight glanced around and saw several blocks of obsidian missing in the walls that ringed the castle. Morgana was right!

"Where's Crafter and Digger?" Stitcher asked.

"They couldn't stop them, so they went with them, hoping to help," the old woman explained. "But I doubt that will do any good. All we have left here are the very young and the very old . . . not much help in battle."

Gameknight glanced at his friends and then stared down at the ground, fear filling his eyes.

"I can't do this alone," he muttered to himself.

Suddenly, someone punched him in the shoulder. Looking up, he found Stitcher glaring at him.

"Who said you were alone?" she asked with a scowl.

"You know what I mean," he explained. "Just us four, we aren't enough to pull off what I have in mind. We need more people, and four or five of us alone can't save all our friends in the Nether."

Just then, Morgana reached over and opened the second door. Inside the keep were another thirty or more NPCs: the old and infirm and young left over from the many villagers that had answered Butch's call for help.

"Butch wouldn't take any of these villagers with him. He said they were too old and couldn't fight." Many of the NPCs behind her took a step forward.

"Maybe we can't swing a sword, but we can help," Morgana said, her eyes burning with confidence. "What do you have in mind?"

"I do have a plan," Gameknight said. "But it's going to be dangerous, and if it doesn't work, we're all going to be in serious trouble."

"What else is new?" Hunter said with a smile.

Gameknight looked at Herder and nodded. The young boy pulled out a hoe and took off for the pumpkin patch in the village. Then he glanced at Snowbrin and smiled.

"Here's what we're gonna do . . ."

CHAPTER 27
GAMEKNIGHT'S SURPRISE

Gameknight999 handed out the splash potions of fire resistance to each villager as they gathered around the Nether portal. They had enough for each NPC to carry a dozen of the fragile bottles, one for themselves and eleven for the other NPCs already in the Nether. They each also carried a bow and multiple stacks of arrows, so that they could fight the blazes from a distance rather than standing toe-to-toe with the fiery creatures.

A select few, including Hunter, Stitcher, and Herder, carried many more potions. They had a special task, a critical one, and all their fates, maybe even the fate of Minecraft itself, depended on their success.

"Is everyone ready?" Gameknight asked.

The NPCs around him all nodded their heads. At the back of the chamber were young children. Topper and Filler, Digger's twins, stood with the young ones, wooden toy swords in their hands. They waved their weapons to Gameknight, signifying that they would be OK. He knew the twins would watch over the other children.

"I'm sure you are all afraid," the User-that-is-not-a-user said. "I'd be concerned if you weren't. You'll be shocked at how hot it is in the Nether, but remember: whatever you do, don't stop. Moving targets are much harder to hit, so always keep going. As soon as Snowbrin does his thing and we begin the attack, start throwing the splash potions on the other villagers. When our friends are protected from the fireballs, then back off and wait for my signal. Does everyone understand?"

The old villagers stood tall and tried to appear confident, but Gameknight999 could see the fear and uncertainty in their eyes.

I hope they all survive, he thought. *I don't know if I could handle it if one of them was hurt because of me.*

"Let's get this party started!" Hunter howled.

The other villagers cheered, some of them raising their bows over their heads.

"OK, then, let's do this," the User-that-is-not-a-user said.

Gameknight999 was the first to step through the portal. His vision was suddenly filled with a wavering purple field that slowly morphed into images of burning netherrack. The heat of the Nether struck him hard in the face. No matter how many times he visited the Nether, he was always shocked by how hot it was. Catching his breath, he moved to the side to allow the others to pass through the magical gateway. With his enchanted bow out, the User-that-is-not-a-user scanned the rusty terrain for any monsters nearby. The occasional zombie-pigman moaned as it shuffled along, but there were no blazes or ghasts or wither skeletons in sight.

So far, they'd been lucky.

More villagers poured out of the portal and moved to the left and right, spreading out and taking cover behind piles of netherrack. Hunter, Stitcher, Herder, and Snowbrin were the last to arrive. Then, with everyone safely gathered, the rag-tag NPC army stared out at the landscape before them.

In the distance stood a huge Nether fortress. Its raised walkways and tall pillars of dark stone spread across the burning landscape like a dark spider web. At the center of the structure was a massive building looming high over the landscape, dwarfing anyone or anything nearby.

Adjacent to the fortress was the Great Lava Ocean. The massive body of molten stone stretched out far into the haze, the opposite shore too far away to be seen. Clustered near the shoreline, Gameknight spotted a large group of NPCs. They huddled close to each other, as a ring of floating blazes slowly closed in on them from all sides. It was Butch's army!

Gameknight could tell one of the blazes was shouting something at the villagers; most likely, that was Charybdis, the blaze king. His words were unintelligible, though, the distance too great. One of the NPCs (most likely Butch, though it was hard to be certain through all the smoke and ash) stepped forward, iron sword held up high. Suddenly, a white-hot ball of fire streaked down from the monster and hit the ground directly in front of the stocky NPC. The ground melted before Butch, changing from the rusty netherrack to a square of lava. This made the NPCs jump back in fright. Butch glanced back at the other villagers and then placed his sword on the ground in front of him. The other villagers did the same, surrendering their weapons and dropping them to their feet.

"There they are," Herder said. "Down by the lava ocean. And they're in trouble."

Gameknight nodded, then turned and faced his own army of aged villagers.

"Let's go, fast and quiet," he said. "They're surrounded. We probably only have minutes before the blazes open fire. Everybody run!"

Gameknight charged forward with Hunter and Stitcher at his side, Herder just two strides behind. Snowbrin shot past them, silently gliding on blocks of snow that trailed behind him like a frozen streamer.

The light-crafter slid across the Nether and went as close to the mass of blazes as he dared, then suddenly veered to the right. Streaking across the netherrack, Snowbrin left a long line of snow blocks in his wake. After he'd traveled maybe fifty blocks, he turned around and laid another trail of blocks right next to the first.

By now, the others had reached the blocks of snow. Herder placed a pumpkin next to each pair of snow blocks. When the orange fruit touched the cubes of snow, they instantly transformed into snowmen, complete with six dark buttons and two sticks for arms. But as soon as the icy creatures stood, they began to flash red as the heat of the Nether tore into them. Fortunately, Hunter and Stitcher were right there behind them, throwing their fire resistance potions against the snowmen's stacked bodies to keep them from taking damage.

Gameknight held his breath as he watched the glass bottles smash against the snowmen.

Orange swirls started to float around the snowmen. And then suddenly, the flashing stopped; with the potions, the snowmen were now impervious to the heat of the Nether.

Now at least we have a chance! he thought.

"Everyone . . . attack!" the User-that-is-not-a-user yelled. "FOR MINECRAFT!"

CHAPTER 28

SNOWBALL FIGHT IN THE NETHER

Snowballs flew through the air and smashed into the blazes. The monsters flashed red with damage, and the sound of metallic clanking filled the air. The blazes slowly turned to face this new threat. Their internal flames sputtered as a second volley of icy spheres crashed into their glowing bodies. Gameknight sprinted forward, firing his bow. He leapt over a narrow river of lava as he fired three quick shots at a nearby blaze, silencing it forever.

"Snowmen . . . in the Nether?" Charybdis asked. "Impossible!"

Gameknight saw the blaze king scan the battlefield. Then his gaze fixed on him, and the monster's eyes filled with venomous hatred.

"It's Gameknight999!" the king of the blazes shouted. "GET HIM!"

The hovering blazes turned to look for the User-that-is-not-a-user, but a third wave of snowballs was launched at the same time. A nearby blaze flared bright, then fired a trio of flaming balls at Gameknight. He quickly rolled to the side, then drew an arrow and notched it to his string as he stood. Firing quickly, the User-that-is-not-a-user launched three shots at the monster. The first two struck home, but the third missed. Its internal flame grew bright again as it readied another attack, but two flaming arrows streaked up into the air from the left and struck the monster simultaneously, taking the last of its HP.

Gameknight didn't look to see who had helped him; he already knew it was Hunter and Stitcher.

"Blazes, forget the snowmen," Charybdis commanded. "Fire at the villagers!"

The monsters turned their backs on the frozen attackers and allowed the balls of ice to smash into them. Each impact was accompanied by a clanking sound as they lost HP. Ignoring the damage, the blazes launched their balls of fire down upon the NPCs, hitting the defenseless villagers.

Screams of pain and terror floated up out of the clustered NPCs. Some of them instantly vanished with a *pop* as multiple fireballs struck them, while others flashed red and took damage as they screamed out in agony.

"NOOOO!" Gameknight cried.

He sprinted toward the villagers, throwing splash potions as he ran. The glass bottles hit the back of their heads and shattered. Orange liquid flew through the air and coated many of them, causing bright orange swirls to rise above their heads. Running around the collection of villagers, Gameknight kept on throwing potions until he'd covered the entire group and depleted his supply, then he skidded to a stop and drew his enchanted bow again.

Another wave of fireballs rained down. Many called out in terror, but this time there were no cries of pain, just gasps of surprise.

"It's fire resistance!" Gameknight said as he made his way through them. "Fight back! Draw your bows and fire before the potion runs out."

Many of the NPCs turned. When they saw it was Gameknight999 standing with them, they stood up a little taller, and a look of determination pushed the fear from their eyes. They bent down and retrieved their weapons, then picked a target up in the sky.

Arrows streaked upward from the ground as the shock of being attacked by the blazes was replaced with courage and rage. Those without bows used pieces of extra armor as shields and protected those around them. Some even used their swords to swing at the fireballs, hoping to knock them back at the attacker. Gameknight watched with pride as the villagers fought hard to defend Minecraft.

Pushing his way through the crowd, he found Digger stooped down, helping an NPC to his feet. Gameknight999 was shocked to see a black smock with a long gray stripe showing from between armored plates. One side of the armor was badly burned, the sleeve of the smock still smoldering.

"Crafter!" Gameknight exclaimed.

"I'm OK," the young NPC grimaced as he was helped to his feet. "Just a little burnt." He glanced at Gameknight and smiled. "I knew you'd make it here, eventually. But for a while there, I wasn't sure we were going to survive. You came just in time. Without you, Gameknight999, we would all be dead."

"They should have taken the time to listen to you," Digger admitted. He pointed to Butch, who was firing his arrows at blazes while their balls of fire fell down upon him like rain. "*He* should have listened to you."

"What happened?" the User-that-is-not-a-user asked.

"They had a trap waiting for us," Digger explained. "Butch charged down toward the fortress, but when we reached it, blazes came out of those caves back there." He pointed to the tunnels carved into the netherrack hills that stood nearby. "In seconds, we were surrounded. You should have been leading this attack, not that reckless Butch."

"It doesn't matter who leads and who follows," Gameknight said. "I understand that now. All that matters is that our people are safe. Each of us has our own strength. Mine is coming up with crazy ideas to help us to defend Minecraft." He pointed to the snowmen. Crafter and Digger both smiled. "Butch's strength is in being a leader, though sometimes his judgment is clouded by his desire for revenge. Right now, though, all we need to focus on is finishing off Charybdis and getting out of here before this battle gets out of control."

"Right," Digger said. "But what about all these blazes?"

Picking up his dual pickaxes, he let out a bellowing cry that seemed to echo across the entire Nether. "VILLAGERS . . . ATTACK!"

The NPCs cheered, and instead of clustering together like frightened children, they surged forward, closing the distance between themselves and their attackers. Arrows streaked up at the monsters, piercing internal flames and chipping away at blaze rods.

The snowmen now advanced and mixed in with the villagers. Their snowballs were like a constant stream of frozen projectiles, viciously smashing into the blazes—payback for the ancient atrocity committed by the fiery monsters. Though they were not very good shots, the volume of snowballs was overpowering. The air was filled with the metallic clanking of wounded blazes as their golden rods fell all around the villagers.

"We might just survive this," Crafter said as he fired his own bow at a floating monster.

"I don't like it," Gameknight said over the din of battle. "It seems like Charybdis is using up all his blazes . . . he must know that he can't win like this. He has something else planned. We should pull back."

"Pull back?" a voice bellowed.

It was Butch. The big NPC was now behind him.

"We are winning, everyone!" Butch exclaimed.

The NPCs cheered.

"Now we should push forward and eliminate the blazes!"

The villagers shouted their excitement and moved forward behind Butch, firing their bows up into the air.

"No . . . NO!" Gameknight screamed.

But the NPCs did not listen. They were focused on Butch and lost in the heat of battle. Every villager wanted revenge for the destruction of their homeland, and their need for revenge ruled their minds. They followed Butch, driving the blazes back toward the lava ocean and the huge nether-brick steps that led out of the massive fortress.

Suddenly, all the blazes turned in unison and, instead of returning fire, floated far out over the lava ocean, away from the villagers. At the same time, an eerie rattling sound came from the Nether fortress. It sounded like old dried-out sticks scraping against each other. The noise wormed its way into Gameknight's ears, making his teeth hurt. Many of the NPCs glanced around, wondering what it was, but Gameknight already knew: skeletons.

"Skeletons are coming," Digger said. "Everyone back up."

The villagers stopped their advance and looked toward the dark citadel. From the wide staircase that descended down from the fortress clattered an army of wither skeletons. Their blackened bones seemed to soak up all the light from the glowing ocean of lava, leaving them looking like shadowy specters of their boney Overworld cousins. The dark skeletons moved down the stairs in lockstep, the stone swords they held out before them glistening in the orange fiery light. When they reached the bottom of the stairway, they turned and spread out along the side of the fortress, closing off any avenue of escape.

"What do we do?" someone asked.

"The splash potion won't protect us from their blades," another shouted.

The NPCs began to back away, slowly.

Then, a splashing sound came from the lava ocean. Huge shapes began to emerge, bouncing up and down as they rose from the molten stone. They sprang into the air with a squishing sound, splashing lava into the air. As the molten stone dripped off their huge, cube-like bodies, Gameknight could see a bright inner core within a dark red body.

"Magma cubes!" Crafter shouted. "They're coming out of the lava."

"Everyone back up," Digger said again.

"No, we need to attack!" Butch said.

"NO! I am the User-that-is-not-a-user, and I say NO!" This time Gameknight asserted himself and refused to be ignored. The villagers were shocked by the ferocity in his voice. "We will not attack. You will all do as I say if you want to live!"

The puzzle pieces were tumbling around in his head, the solution just out of sight. And then he saw the ten or twelve villagers that he needed.

Thunk!

One of the puzzle pieces fell into place. Then Gameknight thought about his Grandma GG, and another part of the solution materialized in his head. In an avalanche of possibilities, everything all fell into place in his mind. And at that moment, Gameknight smiled.

"We . . . should attack," Butch sputtered, but the User-that-is-not-a-user just ignored him.

"But there are too many of them!" someone said.

"We can't do it . . ."

"I'm scared . . ."

"Listen to me, all of you," Gameknight said in a softer voice. He put away his weapons and moved to the center of the group, so that all could hear him. "If we panic and give in to our fears, then we lose, and so does Minecraft. That's what Charybdis wants us to do. If we just blindly attack, then the monsters will close in behind us and trap us against the lava ocean. They will drive us into the boiling stone until the last of us are destroyed, and

Minecraft loses again." He turned to look at those behind him, then slowly walked through the army before him, brushing his hands lightly against each NPC's shoulder and back. "We are a family, not a mindless machine of violence. We are calculating and strategic, while the monsters are just thoughtless creatures of destruction. If we are careful and smart, then we can survive this battle."

"We should listen to Gameknight999," one of the villagers said.

"What is your plan?" asked another.

"Yes . . . tell us."

Gameknight glanced back at the Nether fortress. The wither skeletons were still piling out of the fortress, while the magma cubes were bouncing their way onto the shoreline. The other villagers turned to glare at the monsters, but when they turned back, they found the User-that-is-not-a-user smiling.

"Here's what we are going to do . . ."

And as he explained his plan, the villagers, too, began to smile.

CHAPTER 29

GRANDPARENTS' REVENGE

The magma cubes bounced into the air with a squishy sound, a bright fiery glow coming from the center of their dark red bodies. They expanded like an accordion as they jumped up into the air, then compressed back into their cubic shape when they landed on the ground, moving closer with each bounce.

A dozen archers stepped out of the formation and knelt on the ground.

"Aim for a big one, then shoot the smaller ones after they divide," Digger shouted. "FIRE!"

A stream of arrows sailed across the rusty landscape and pierced the large gelatinous cubes. The magma cubes groaned in pain, but continued to bounce toward them. The archers fired again, causing a couple of the bouncing monsters to divide into smaller cubes. More archers stepped forward and fired on the creatures, aiming for the smaller ones. They divided again, into smaller and smaller cubes, until they disappeared with a pop. Turning their attention back to the larger monsters, the villagers worked in groups of three and fired on the same creature, dividing them with a single volley.

As they attacked, Gameknight pulled out his remaining fire resistance potions and threw them on the snowmen that stood near the edge of the lava ocean, giving them a final eight minutes of life before the heat of the Nether would melt them to nothing.

The frozen creatures fired up at the blazes and the burning monsters launched fireballs back at them. Gameknight knew the blazes could just move out over the lava ocean, out of range, and wait until the snowmen just melted, but the ancient hatred between these two creatures was so great that neither could disengage. With the help of the fire resistance potion, the snowmen were slowly winning the battle.

Notching an arrow to his bow, Gameknight now turned his attention to the wither skeletons. The dark monsters were slowly spreading out along the edge of the fortress, but they had not attacked yet. It appeared as if they wanted to wrap around behind the NPCs so that they could trap them between their skeleton swords and the blazes.

Perfect, Gameknight thought with a smile.

"The skeletons are circling around us," Crafter said, his voice cracking with worry.

"I know, that's what I want," Gameknight replied.

"What you *want*?!" exclaimed Butch. "Are you crazy? If they get behind us, we'll have enemies on both sides of us and no way to escape. We should attack them now, before it's too late."

"Butch, I understand what you are saying, but a great general, named Sun Tzu, once said a long time ago: 'All warfare is based on deception',"

Gameknight said. "The skeletons *think* they are putting us into a trap, while in actuality, they are the ones falling into our ambush."

"What are you talking about?" the big NPC asked.

"You will see," the User-that-is-not-a-user replied. "The deception must be complete. Our forces must seem scared to draw them in. You will see our salvation at the same time that the skeletons see their doom."

Gameknight then turned and faced the other villagers.

"Have no fear, friends," the User-that-is-not-a-user said. "There is help nearby, but right now, we must play the part of the victim." He smiled as he scanned their faces.

Some of the warriors nodded their square heads, but still many had their eyes on Butch. Gameknight could tell that they wanted to do as Butch suggested—charge forward and attack. But if they followed the big NPC, then everyone was doomed.

Butch, exasperated, yelled and screamed, shouting about revenge and attacking the skeletons; but as he screamed, more of the warriors noticed Gameknight's calm, confident demeanor.

"Be calm and be patient," Gameknight said in a reassuring voice. "There is help out there . . . just have faith."

This seemed to calm the villagers, but Butch continued to rant and rave; he was itching for a fight.

The skeletons were now behind them, and they began pushing forward.

"Don't be scared . . . stand your ground," Gameknight growled.

"There's too many of them!" Digger cried, and while it sounded to the skeletons like he was scared, Gameknight recognized that there was a hint of acting in his loud voice.

"We should just lay down our weapons and surrender!" Crafter shouted in the same manner, before flashing Gameknight a smile and winking.

The User-that-is-not-a-user just nodded his head and smiled.

"We're so afraid!" Gameknight said in a voice loud enough to be heard by all.

The effect of these words shone clear on the skeletons. They were hungry for a victory and advanced, ignoring everything but the supposed pleas for mercy from the villagers. As a result, while they closed in the NPCs, they didn't hear the footsteps from behind. The dark monsters moved closer to their supposed prey.

"Stitcher, Hunter . . . NOW!" Gameknight yelled.

Suddenly, an angry cry arose from behind the skeletons. The bony monsters turned to see the source of the noise and found an army of grandparents charging toward them, each with an arrow notched to their bow. At the head of the charge were Hunter and Stitcher, their enchanted bows lighting the Nether with a magical blue glow.

They charged forward until they were a dozen blocks away, then stopped and opened fire all at once. Their arrows tore into the skeletons, causing the bony creatures to yell in both surprise and pain.

The dark monsters turned to fight the grandparents, their swords deflecting some of the arrows. That was when Gameknight and the other villagers opened fire with their own weapons. Arrows fell down upon the ashen monsters from both sides, tearing HP from their bony bodies. Uncertain what to do, or which direction to fight, the skeletons stopped and drew into a tight formation, their stone swords deflecting arrows when they could.

Butch started to charge forward, but Digger grabbed him by the back of his armor and yanked him back.

"We can't shoot at them with our bows if you are out there with them," Digger said. "Gameknight has a plan and we're going to stick to it. He can get us out of the Nether . . . alive. I think that's a better idea than just attacking."

Many of the villagers nodded their heads. Gameknight could still see the fire in their eyes. They wanted revenge for the destruction done to the Overworld, but they also knew their situation was precarious, and strategy was better than just reckless attacks. Slowly, the NPCs turned their gazes from Butch to Gameknight999, their faces seeming hopefully attentive.

"Center ranks: keep firing," Gameknight said. "Warriors on the right and left: draw swords and move around to the skeleton's flanks."

One group, led by Digger, broke away from the main body and moved around the side of the skeleton formation. Crafter led the other party, the warriors running across the burning netherrack. Some of the skeletons moved to engage the warriors, but the main body of archers held them back.

When they had the skeletons surrounded, Gameknight pounded his sword upon his chest plate. The clank of diamond against diamond echoed across the Nether, sounding like thunder. The grandparents on either side of the skeletons started banging their bows against their armor, causing more thunder to erupt.

The skeletons turned and glanced nervously to the left and right, unsure what was happening. The archers stopped their attack and now drew swords. They banged on their armor, adding to the cacophony until it was overwhelmingly loud.

The skeletons now were terrified. The villagers advanced slowly, banging on their armor. The noise hammered at the skeletons from all sides, reflecting off the mounds of netherrack and Nether quartz. They didn't know what was happening, and Gameknight could tell their discipline was begging to fall apart.

It was time.

"Butch, I think it's time to do what you want to do," Gameknight said so all could hear.

The big NPC glanced back at Gameknight999, and a smile came to his face.

"Now?" he asked.

The User-that-is-a-user nodded to him and returned a mischievous grin.

"CHARGE!" Butch yelled.

The NPCs all ran forward, swords ready. With the skeletons surrounded and packed into a tight circle, those at the center could do nothing but wait until the skeletons on the outside of the circle had perished. By surrounding them, Gameknight had reduced the number of skeletons they would have to face at one time.

A mighty crash sounded when the two armies met. Gameknight smashed into the skeleton formation with both swords swinging. He was at Butch's side, slashing at skeletons with iron and diamond. The monsters wanted to get at the

User-that-is-not-a-user, but Butch's iron sword combined with Gameknight's own blades kept the creatures back.

With warriors on three sides, and the grandparent archers firing from the rear, the monsters stood little chance of winning. Blades and arrows tore into skeleton HP, causing their bones to clatter to the ground. But they were not the only victims. Many villagers felt the bite of the skeleton swords. Piles of items floated on the ground where NPCs had fallen.

The User-that-is-not-a-user dove into the battle, his two swords cleaving a devastating path of destruction through the skeleton formation. He watched those around him as he fought, helping to block an attacking skeleton sword where he could to allow another NPC to drive home the critical hit. The villagers fought as teams, each helping out the other, while the skeletons just battled as individuals.

Bones and piles of coal began to litter the ground as the warriors pushed harder. Screams of pain from both sides filled the air, but the villagers did not relent; they drove forward, slashing at the dark creatures until every last one of them had been destroyed.

The NPCs cheered, then turned and charged at the magma cubes. Only a half-dozen of the creatures remained, but those did not last much longer, as a hundred arrows fell down upon them. The bouncing cubes divided again and again until they were all destroyed, the ground covered with round balls of yellowish-orange magma cream.

All that was left now were the blazes. Gameknight could see the blaze king, Charybdis, floating far out over the lava ocean, out of range from the snowmen. But the other monster forces had been defeated; it seemed as if the villagers were going to win the day.

Suddenly, one of the snowmen flashed red, then disappeared.

"Did you see that?" Crafter said. "A fireball didn't even hit the snowman . . . it just disappeared."

"The fire resistance potions!" Stitcher said, now at Gameknight's side. "They are wearing off."

"Does anyone have any more?" the User-that-is-not-a-user asked.

Everyone shook their heads.

Another snowman flashed red, then another and another as the frozen warriors melted away; the heat from the Nether was too much for the creatures. As the snowmen fell, the blazes drew closer. They began to throw their fireballs with greater intensity, aiming at the remaining few defenders.

"Come on, we have to go help them," Gameknight shouted. "Charge!"

The NPC army sprinted forward, but they were too far away to help. The last of the snowmen finally expired, leaving Snowbrin on the shore of the Great Lava Ocean, alone. The twenty remaining blazes all fired on the light-crafter at once. As Gameknight watched, it seemed like the flaming balls of death were moving in slow motion. Snowbrin turned and faced Gameknight999 right when the fireballs hit, a look of fear on his white, boxy face.

He disappeared with a *pop*, leaving behind a pile of snowballs that floated just off the ground, bobbing up and down ever so slightly.

Charybdis laughed.

"NO!" the User-that-is-not-a-user yelled.

Fury rose up within Gameknight999. The battle was over, the monsters had lost, and yet they still felt it necessary to take another life. Rage clouded his vision as he glared up at the blazes. The fiery monsters drew closer, but still stayed over the lava ocean, ready to retreat if necessary. Glancing up at the blaze king, Gameknight knew that the blaze threat would never be eliminated until the king was destroyed.

I have to do it, he thought. *I can't let anyone else take the risk of facing that monster in battle. If it's just him and me, then at least my friends will be safe.*

As this realization solidified within his mind, he knew what he needed to do. He had to goad the blaze king into a contest of PvP.

"You are defeated, Charybdis," the User-that-is-not-a-user said. "Come down here and face your punishment. I am judge and jury, and I say you are guilty of crimes against Minecraft."

"Oh really?" the blaze king said. "And what is my punishment?"

Gameknight glanced at the pile of snowballs that had once been held by Snowbrin and growled.

"I will be your executioner," he said. "Come down here and face me in combat, if you are not a coward."

"Gameknight, no!" Crafter shouted.

"All of you, get back!" he yelled. "This is between Charybdis and myself. Everyone give me room, so I can punish this vile creation of Herobrine's for the last time."

The NPCs moved back and let the blaze king draw near. He slowly floated down to the nether-rack ground to face his enemy.

"I may have lost this war, but I will win this battle," the blaze king said.

"You don't have Herobrine to help you this time," Gameknight said. "He saved you once before, but this time, you will be destroyed."

"We shall see," Charybdis said.

"I'm tired of talking with one of Herobrine's dogs," Gameknight spat. "Come on, blaze, let's dance."

CHAPTER 30

GAMEKNIGHT999 VS. CHARYBDIS

Gameknight drew his bow and fired a stream of arrows at the creature. Remembering their last conflict, he focused not on where the blaze king *was* but, rather, where he was *going to be*. He shot arrows all around where Charybdis was, so that no matter where the monster moved, an arrow would find him.

Flash . . . the monster fired a trio of fireballs. Gameknight rolled to the left, just as the burning spheres smashed to the ground. The intense heat of the fireballs was something he didn't expect. Each flaming ball made the ground glow brighter and brighter until the third fireball turned the spot into lava.

Fear rippled through Gameknight999. These new fireballs were terrifying; they were much hotter than anything he'd ever faced before.

But Charybdis is not the only one in this battle with a few surprises, Gameknight thought.

Moving along the lava ocean shore, Gameknight backed away from the blaze king, shooting at the monster while dodging the white-hot fireballs. More small pools of lava began to form across the ground as the burning spheres smashed into the landscape. He had to do something different, or Charybdis was going to change all of the land to lava.

Gameknight was almost to his destination. Drawing an arrow from his inventory, he fired, then drew and fired, then drew and fired again. As the arrows flew toward their target, the User-that-is-not-a-user retreated to where Snowbrin had died. The icy light-crafter's inventory flowed into Gameknight999, making him smile.

"What are you grinning at, fool?" Charybdis asked.

Gameknight said nothing. Instead, he sprinted away from the lava ocean in a zigzag path, the blaze king following close behind. Fireballs crashed all around him as he ran, but he was moving too erratically for the monster to score a direct hit.

Finally, a fireball came close, scraping against his leg, causing pain to shoot up his side. He flashed red with damage as his HP dropped. The heat of the fireball was indescribable. Agony surged through his nerves as his leg throbbed.

Turning, Gameknight fired another volley of arrows, aiming around the blaze instead of directly at him. Two more arrows hit, causing his enemy to flash red.

Another trio of fireballs rocketed down at him. Gameknight moved to the right, but this time, Charybdis had spread out his shots. The balls of fire landed to the right *and* left of his position, smashing into the ground with the force of a blacksmith's hammer. One of the balls struck Gameknight directly in the chest. The heat was mostly absorbed by his diamond armor, but some of it still made it through. It felt as if someone had poured molten metal on him; the pain was nearly overwhelming.

A loud crack sounded. Gameknight reached up and felt a wide fissure in his chest plate. That fireball had nearly consumed his armor. One more like that and the diamond chest plate would be worthless, which meant the User-that-is-not-a-user would be in grave danger.

Putting away his bow, Gameknight sprinted directly toward the monster. A look of shock covered the flaming monster's face as he watched the User-that-is-not-a-user unexpectedly approach. Suddenly, Gameknight pulled out the snowballs that Snowbrin had dropped when he died. Throwing them with all his strength, he launched an icy attack at the monster.

Charybdis moved upward, away from the threat, but the snowball's range was still great. The chilly attack landed multiple hits on the monster, causing the creature's internal flame to sputter for a moment. But then the monster's flame grew bright when he launched a counterattack. Fireballs rained down around Gameknight as he backed up again, throwing the last of the snowballs that he had at the blaze king. One more hit Charybdis, but the monster still had enough of his internal fire to fight back.

As he retreated, Gameknight tripped over the edge of a netherrack block and fell backward. Instantly, Charybdis pounced, heaving more of the deadly spheres down upon him. Gameknight rolled to the left as one of the balls smashed on the ground, then rolled again to the right, missing the second flaming ball. But as he stood, the third fireball struck him square in the chest.

Pain blasted every nerve as a burning sensation flowed across his body. A loud crack sounded as the last bit of his diamond armor fell to the ground in pieces; he was defenseless.

Charybdis laughed with malicious glee as he fired another volley of fireballs at his victim. Gameknight watched the glowing balls approach in slow motion, fear overwhelming his mind. But just before they hit, Butch stepped in front of him. The first fireball struck the big NPC in the shoulder. But with his sword, he batted away the next two, causing the spheres of death to fly back toward the blaze king. The flaming monster dodged the fireballs by moving to the left and allowing them to just miss.

"Butch, thank you," the User-that-is-not-a-user said. "You saved my life."

"Let's just get this done," the big NPC said as he pulled Gameknight to his feet. "I'll be your armor . . . ATTACK!"

The User-that-is-not-a-user nodded and charged toward the monster with Butch directly in front of him. The big NPC batted away most of the fireballs that fell down on them, using his body as a shield for Gameknight999. With his bow humming, the User-that-is-not-a-user fired a continuous stream of arrows at the monster.

Flash . . . red. An arrow found its target.

Grunt . . . red. A fireball hit Butch.

The big NPC staggered for a moment, then continued to charge forward, cutting away at the fireballs that fell near. Gameknight could see cracks running along Butch's iron armor; it would not withstand many more hits. But it was also clear that Charybdis was near death. The monster's flame was dimming and flickering with uncertainty. All three of the battling warriors were near death, and the outcome of this battle could still go in any direction.

Another of Gameknight's arrows struck the blaze king just as the monster fired a volley of white-hot balls. The impact of the arrow caused the first two fireballs to veer wide to the right, but the third one fell straight on them, hitting Butch in the stomach. His iron armor shattered as he fell to his knees and collapsed.

"NO!" Gameknight shouted as he drew an arrow back and fired.

When he released the shot, his enchanted bow shattered, its strength finally consumed.

Dropping to the ground, he grabbed Butch and held him for a moment.

"Don't stop . . . destroy the blaze," Butch coughed. "If he gets to the lava ocean he will be healed . . . get him now!"

Gameknight knew he was right. Carefully, he set the big NPC on the ground, then drew his sword and shield. The blaze was surprised to see the shield; he'd probably never seen one before, as they were new from a recent software update.

Gameknight advanced as the blaze threw balls of death down upon him, the burning attack smashing into his shield with the force of a giant's fist. He could feel the heat building up on the shield, the center beginning to glow bright. It wouldn't last long until it—

Crack! The shield shattered into tiny shards and fell around his feet.

This was it. Gameknight knew that if the blaze landed just one hit, he was dead. He had to time everything perfectly, so that the monster wouldn't have time to avoid his attack; but if he timed it wrong himself . . . then he didn't have a chance.

Charbydis's internal flame suddenly blossomed and grew bright, obscuring the monster's vision for just an instant. Gameknight quickly rolled to the side, then threw his diamond sword at the monster with all his might. The enchanted weapon tumbled end over end through the air. It seemed to Gameknight999 as if it were moving in slow motion. Charybdis attacked, his fireballs bursting into life, streaking down at the spot where Gameknight999 had been standing. Just as the second fireball shot through the air, Gameknight's sword struck home, hitting the blaze king in the chest. He flashed red one last time, and an expression of shock came over his glowing face as the realization of his demise filled his mind.

Charybdis tried to say something to Gameknight, probably one last insult, but he disappeared before the words could form. He vanished with a *pop*, his blaze rods falling to the ground alongside Gameknight's sword. The few blazes that had survived the battle with the snowmen, seeing their leader destroyed, rose high into the air and fled into the haze of the Nether.

Charybdis, the blaze king, was dead.

CHAPTER 31

BUTCH

A cheer rose up into the air as the villagers celebrated their unlikely victory.

"We did it!" they shouted.

"Gameknight999!"

"The User-that-is-not-a-user saved us!"

"Gameknight and Butch destroyed the blaze king!"

Oh no, Gameknight thought. *Butch!*

Gameknight turned and saw the big NPC still lying on the ground, his breathing labored. He sprinted to him and knelt at his side. Black tendrils of smoke rose from his smoldering clothes like magical snakes taking flight. He patted the still-burning sections with his blocky hands, then pulled out a flask of water and offered it to his friend.

"No, water will do me no good," Butch coughed. "My fate is sealed. I can feel the last of my HP slipping away and I know what is in store for me."

"Butch, you saved me and helped me destroy Charybdis. You saved a lot of people with your sacrifice," Gameknight said.

The big NPC coughed.

"You were right, my thirst for vengeance just left me feeling empty," Butch said. "I led these villagers down here and they were almost destroyed because of my need for revenge. But you saved them with your plan. You thought, while I just reacted. Gameknight999 is the true protector of Minecraft, and I am nothing but an empty shell."

"No, you are not an empty shell. Your sacrifice to protect me saved all these people and saved Minecraft. If you hadn't stepped in front of me, Charybdis would have won, and his reign of fire would have devoured the Overworld. You did what you said you'd do: protect Minecraft with every fiber of your being . . ."

Butch coughed again. "I guess I did, didn't I?" he said as a smile formed across his boxy face.

He took one more strained breath and peered up at Gameknight999 with a look of contentment on his face. Then, with a *pop*, he disappeared, his items littering the ground. Gameknight felt a presence behind him, and glanced over his shoulder, tears streaming down his square cheeks.

All of the villagers stood behind him, with Crafter and Hunter at the front of the group. Gameknight could feel tears evaporating off his cheeks from the heat of the Nether. He was overcome with grief at seeing Butch die. That villager had been a mountain of strength and courage, something that Minecraft needed. But as Gameknight looked at those around him, he realized that all of these NPCs had the same strength and courage, for those traits did not come from muscles and size, but rather from within. And all of the villagers had seen the strength of character in Butch, and they now carried his memory . . . and his courage.

Gameknight stood and raised his hand, fingers spread wide, then clenched his hand into a fist as tiny square tears tumbled down his cheeks. He squeezed his hand tight as he closed his eyes, trying the crush the grief from his heart, but all he did was cry harder at the loss he felt in his soul.

A gentle hand settled onto his shoulder. Opening his eyes, Gameknight found Hunter gazing up at him, her red hair glowing like a crimson halo in the fiery light of the Nether.

"It's time to go home," she said softly.

He nodded and lowered his hand, then started to head back to the portal. They walked in silence across the Nether, the only sound coming from the moaning zombie-pigmen, who had been oblivious to the battle that had just been fought on the shore of the Great Lava Ocean. The villagers scanned the skies for more blazes, but the flaming creatures had lost the will to fight after the defeat of their king.

When he reached the portal, he stared back down at the Nether fortress and the glowing ocean. He could see the exact spot where Butch had perished and thought, *I should come back some day and build a monument to him. Maybe something made out of packed ice.*

The villagers began to step through the portal, teleporting back to the Overworld, while Gameknight stood next to the magical gateway. Hunter moved to his side, silent and contemplative. Crafter and Digger stayed back as well and waited as the rest of the villagers stepped through the portal. Finally, Stitcher and Herder approached, the two young

NPCs walking with the grandparent army, making sure everyone made it.

Once all the elderly had gone through the gateway, the six friends glanced at each other solemnly.

"He gave his life for me," Gameknight said as tears began to tumble down his cheeks again. "I've seen lots of people perish in Minecraft, but none of them had ever knowingly sacrificed their life so that I could survive."

"It was a noble act that we will all remember for the rest of our lives," Crafter said.

"But who's to say that my life was more important than his?" Gameknight asked. "I don't understand."

"It isn't for us to understand what Butch was thinking," Hunter said. "All we can do is live our lives the best we can, helping as many people as possible, so that we can continue to be worthy of his sacrifice."

"Hunter is right," Crafter added. "Butch did what he said he wanted to do: protect Minecraft and the lives of every villager. He gave the last ounce of his life to do that. The only way we can thank him is to make the most of the life Butch has given us and do good deeds . . . no, *great* deeds. We must be worthy of his decision and his selfless act."

"Agreed," the six companions said in unison.

"You know," Gameknight said with a sigh as he turned to look at Crafter and Digger. "I thought the villagers stopped needing me, that they needed Butch more. It seemed like all the villagers wanted to follow Butch. I felt unnecessary and insignificant."

"We never stopped needing you, Gameknight," Crafter said. "Maybe we just took you for granted and figured you would always be there for us. We were wrong. We should have let you know how special you are to us, and we're sorry."

"Yeah . . . there is no replacing the king of the griefers, no matter how hard we try," Digger said with a smile. "You will always be a part of all our families."

"That's right," Hunter added. "And you won't forget it again, if you know what's good for you!"

"OK," Gameknight replied sheepishly. "I guess I was just feeling insecure."

"You should never doubt your value to your friends," Stitcher added.

"Yeah," Herder said. "Look around at the people you help. They are living happy lives because of the many times you've helped everyone. It's easy to forget that people care about you, and it's easy to feel alone . . . I know that better than anyone else. But I've learned to judge myself by the friends I keep, and you should do the same."

Gameknight nodded his head, a smile creeping onto his face.

"Good talk," Hunter said sarcastically, "but maybe we should get out of the Nether before the monsters change their mind and come back to crush us."

"That's a great idea," Crafter added. "Let's get out of here."

One at a time, the companions stepped through the portal, Gameknight and Hunter waiting to be last.

Pulling out a block of TNT, Gameknight placed it next to the portal, and then quickly built a redstone circuit that would give them a few seconds before the red-striped block exploded and destroyed the portal.

"You ready?" Gameknight asked.

Hunter nodded her head.

"Maybe we should stop visiting the Nether," Hunter said with a smile. "It never seems to be very much fun."

"Agreed," Gameknight replied, then placed the redstone torch next to the circuit.

Instantly, the redstone turned bright red as the delay circuit started to work. They stepped through the portal together, and as they materialized in Gameknight's castle, they could hear the echo of an explosion from the wavering purple teleportation field. Then it winked out.

Moving out of the room, Gameknight took the stairs down to the ground level, then quickly climbed a ladder that led to the top of the obsidian wall that ringed his fortress. He found many of the villagers up there, glaring out at the devastated forest that surrounded their community.

He glanced around for Crafter and found the young NPC standing off to the right. Gameknight moved to his side.

"What are we going to do about the destroyed forest?" Crafter asked, his blue eyes filled with doubt.

"We're going to replant," Gameknight said. "You still have tons of bones from past battles with skeletons . . . right?"

Crafter nodded.

"Good. Here's what we're going to do," Gameknight explained. "We are going to find a forest that has not been burned, then trim the leaves until we find some saplings. Then we're going to dig up the dirt that has been changed to glass and replace it with fresh dirt." His voice rose in volume so the other villagers could hear. "We're going to replant this forest, then we're going to replant the next forest and the one after that, until the damage to Minecraft has been repaired. We'll use the bone meal from the skeleton bones to make the trees grow faster. It will take a while, but we'll get the forests back to how they were."

He put a hand on Crafter's shoulder and peered down at the young NPC.

"We will do what Butch would do: attack this problem head-on and not give up until the task is complete. You agree?"

Crafter glared out at all the dead trees that were lying on their sides, blackened and charred, then looked back up at Gameknight999. With his blue eyes growing brighter, he nodded his head.

"Let's do this," Crafter said.

"Come on, everyone, we have some forests to rebuild," Gameknight said as he headed to the ground level.

The User-that-is-not-a-user ran out of his castle and across the grassy plain, heading for the charred forest. He glanced to his right and saw Hunter and Stitcher running on his right, Crafter and Digger on his left. Behind him, he could hear Herder's wolves howling with excitement. Glancing over his shoulder, he saw that the entire village was running in his wake, many of the NPCs with pickaxes and shovels in their hands.

Gameknight glanced at his friends, and realized the truth in Herder's words back in the Nether. He had great friends around him, and realized that they had always been there for him. He was honored to be among them and felt important because of their presence. It didn't matter if he was leading or following; all that mattered was that they were together.

"OK, everyone," the User-that-is-not-a-user shouted. "Let's build us a forest!"

The NPCs all cheered with excitement.

"Come on, forest," Gameknight muttered in a low voice, a smile creeping across his square. "Let's dance."

MINECRAFT SEEDS

All of the different biomes and structures mentioned in the book can be seen on Gameknight999's server. Just go to the book warp room on the survival server and you'll see the buttons for each chapter. You can use the command */warp bookwarps*. I'll be building the creeper hives somewhere on the server so that all of you can see what I was imagining while I was writing. Maybe I'll try to make one of the burned-out forests as well, if that's possible . . . come to the server and find out.

For those without access to the server, I've listed Minecraft seeds for version 1.87. I don't know if they will work with Minecraft PE or if they'll work for version 1.9; you'll just have to try them out and see.

NOTE FROM THE AUTHOR

I've been receiving some really fantastic stories from readers all over the world. Thank you all for submitting them to me through www.markcheverton.com. They are really incredible, and the creativity that is being exhibited through these stories is wonderful. You don't have to write about Minecraft to get it posted on my website—you just have to write. So keep creating and keep the stories coming; I am always excited to see them in my email.

I had a great time writing this book, but it was, for some reason, really difficult to get finished. I don't know why. Maybe playing Minecraft too much distracted me—I'm sure that didn't help. But one thing that *did* help was seeing all the incredibly creative buildings and inventions that have been popping up on the Gameknight999 Minecraft server; it was very motivating and exciting.

One interesting thing I've noticed, which I've never seen on any other servers, is the way kids play *together* on the Gameknight999 network. Usually when people start playing on a new server in Minecraft, they run far away from spawn so they can build their home. They try to hide in their little hidey-hole or stone house or castle away from others in order to avoid being griefed, which means they end up playing alone or maybe only with a trusted friend. But on Gameknight999's server, kids seem to want to play together in large communities. They build their fantastic houses near each other and build roads connecting them to other kids. Shops are created so that players can trade things like diamonds for player's heads (I wonder what a Monkeypants_271 head is worth?) or trade gold for minecarts, etc.

It seems that kids on this server really work *together* rather than as individuals, which has caused huge cities to grow that include collaborative play and role-playing adventures. This is rare on Minecraft servers—and I think it is extraordinary. It is my hope that a small part of this is because of Gameknight999 and Crafter and Hunter and all my characters. Maybe my books are creating this atmosphere of trust and cooperation, maybe just a little . . . I hope.

You can see images of some of the great things that are being created by going to www.gameknight999.com. You can submit images of your own creations to me through that website or through www.markcheverton.com, and they will be posted with the other images. And I will also tell you a little secret: if you go onto the survival server, you might just find some new book covers hidden amongst the trees, or in the desert, or maybe in Crafter's village.

Quadbamber (LBEGaming on YouTube) has been instrumental in helping us make the Gameknight999 Minecraft server such a great—and safe—place for kids. His knowledge of servers is legendary, and we are lucky to have him working with us. If you see him on the server, be sure to say hello.

If you see Gameknight999 or myself, Monkeypants_271, on the server, challenge us to a game of spleef, or paintball, or TNT-Defense. I have to warn you, though, I'm terrible at mini games and most likely you will win. Come build and create and help others, and, of course, watch out for creepers.

Mark

AVAILABLE NOW FROM MARK CHEVERTON AND SKY PONY PRESS

THE GAMEKNIGHT999 SERIES
The world of Minecraft comes to life in this thrilling adventure!

Gameknight999 loved Minecraft, and above all else, he loved to grief—to intentionally ruin the gaming experience for other users.

But when one of his father's inventions teleports him into the game, Gameknight is forced to live out a real-life adventure inside a digital world. What will happen if he's killed? Will he respawn? Die in real life? Stuck in the game, Gameknight discovers Minecraft's best-kept secret, something not even the game's programmers realize: the creatures within the game are alive! He will have to stay one step ahead of the sharp claws of zombies and pointed fangs of spiders, but he'll also have to learn to make friends and work as a team if he has any chance of surviving the Minecraft war his arrival has started.

With deadly endermen, ghasts, and dragons, this action-packed trilogy introduces the heroic Gameknight999 and has proven to be a runaway publishing smash, showing that the Gameknight999 series is the perfect companion for Minecraft fans of all ages.

Invasion of the Overworld (Book One):
$9.99 paperback • 978-1-63220-711-1

Battle for the Nether (Book Two):
$9.99 paperback • 978-1-63220-712-8

Confronting the Dragon (Book Three):
$9.99 paperback • 978-1-63450-046-3

AVAILABLE NOW FROM MARK CHEVERTON
AND SKY PONY PRESS

  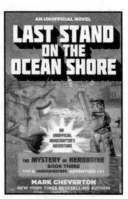

THE MYSTERY OF HEROBRINE SERIES
Gameknight999 must save his friends from an evil virus intent on destroying all of Minecraft!

Gameknight999 was sucked into the world of Minecraft when one of his father's inventions went haywire. Trapped inside the game, the former griefer learned the error of his ways, transforming into a heroic warrior and defeating powerful endermen, ghasts, and dragons to save the world of Minecraft and his NPC friends who live in it.

Gameknight swore he'd never go inside Minecraft again. But that was before Herobrine, a malicious virus infecting the very fabric of the game, threatened to destroy the entire Overworld and escape into the real world. To outsmart an enemy much more powerful than any he's ever faced, the User-that-is-not-a-user will need to go back into the game, where real danger lies around every corner. From zombie villages and jungle temples to a secret hidden at the bottom of a deep ocean, the action-packed adventures of Gameknight999 and his friends (and, now, family) continue in this thrilling follow-up series for Minecraft fans of all ages.

Trouble in Zombie-town (Book One):
$9.99 paperback • 978-1-63450-094-4

The Jungle Temple Oracle (Book Two):
$9.99 paperback • 978-1-63450-096-8

Last Stand on the Ocean Shore (Book Three):
$9.99 paperback • 978-1-63450-098-2

EXCERPT FROM SYSTEM OVERLOAD

A BRAND NEW GAMEKNIGHT999 ADVENTURE

They walked across the savannah through the rest of the day and into the night. A few spiders tried to approach the villagers, but the wolves had keen eyesight and spotted the monsters from far away. The gigantic arachnids never made it close enough for the army to even see them.

By the time the moon was high overhead, the zombie had led them to a large hill, a dark cave carved into its base.

"Zombie-town is through there," the monster said with a moan.

Gameknight moved to the mouth of the cave and peered inside. It was pitch black in the passage, and monsters could be hiding anywhere. He had a bad feeling about this. Stepping away from the cave, he moved to Crafter's side.

"I don't like this," the User-that-is-not-a-user said.

"I know. Neither do I," the young NPC said.

"Why is this monster helping us anyway?" Hunter asked in a low voice. "Zombies hate us more than just about anything in the world. It makes no sense that this one would show us where the prisoners were taken."

"Maybe the zombie thinks there would be nothing we'd be able to do to help them," Digger suggested.

"Or maybe it just wanted to prolong his life," Cobbler added. He had quietly snuck up behind Crafter and was now standing at his side. "He probably figured that he'd be killed right there if he didn't help. So he led us here to keep himself alive."

"We wouldn't have done that," Gameknight said. "We don't murder in cold blood."

"It's just a zombie," Cobbler said in a low voice. "They probably did something to my village as well . . . who cares what happens to it?"

"*I* care," Gameknight said pointedly. "We aren't going to murder that zombie."

"Great, just my luck," Cobbler replied, then sulked and walked away.

"Cobbler does raises an important point," Crafter said. "It's possible that the zombie is just scared, and willing to do anything to stay alive."

"Well, let's see how much he's willing to help," Gameknight said.

He stood and walked straight toward the monster. As he neared, he drew his diamond sword. The zombie stood, fear painted across his scarred face.

"You got us here. Now we don't need you anymore," Gameknight said.

"No, the user is wrong," the zombie said. "Many tunnels down there. Only a zombie can find the correct path."

"You lie," Gameknight snapped. "And you've probably set a trap for us to walk into. There are probably zombies waiting for us in that tunnel right now."

"No, zombies do not guard the tunnel," the monster pleaded. "It is not necessary, as this is a secret entrance. Only zombies know about it. There might be spiders and creepers hiding, but this zombie cannot control that. Zombies will not be in the tunnels. They are in zombie-town."

"Well, maybe we'll keep you alive a bit longer," the User-that-is-not-a-user growled as convincingly as he could. He turned and winked at Crafter, then glared at the monster. "Show us the way, before I lose patience."

The monster moved quickly to the entrance, then walked into the tunnel. Digger had to run forward and grab the end of the rope before the monster moved too far ahead. He yanked back on the rope, pulling the monster with it.

"Wait," Digger ordered.

The zombie stopped in his tracks and stood, motionless.

"Herder, wolves to the front and back of the army," Gameknight ordered. "Everyone keep your eyes open. Place torches only on the right side of the tunnel. Let's move out."

The army moved forward with the zombie at the head of the formation, wolves on either side. The monster led them through the twisting and turning passage. It intersected with different tunnels and passed through multiple large caverns, each with multiple exits. It was like a labyrinth. Gameknight almost expected to find the Minotaur waiting for them, but thankfully that was Greek mythology and not Minecraft. He now understood why the zombies didn't bother to guard the entrance. Without insider help, there was no hope that the villagers would have ever found the correct path.

Finally, they reached a tall chamber with a stream of lava flowing into a gentle pool of water. A sheet of black obsidian formed where the two liquids clashed. Across from the dark plane, an unusually flat wall stood tall in the orange light of the molten stone, with a single block of stone that stuck out of it.

"There . . . the block," the zombie moaned. "Push it."

Gameknight remembered this kind of entrance from when he had to rescue his sister, Monet113, from the zombie-town near Crafter's village.

Moving to the block, he pushed on the stone. It moved just the slightest bit. Instantly the walls begin to shake and the sound of stone grinding against stone filled the air. Slowly, a section of the stone wall began to slide sideways, revealing a dark passage that led into another chamber.

Gameknight ran forward before the rocky door was done moving, dashing inside. The orange light from the nearby lava stream provided just enough light to see the ground, making it possible for him to avoid any holes.

When he reached the end of the passage, he stopped and hid in the shadowy entrance. Before him lay a gigantic cave filled with homes of different size and shape. Each seemed as if they were build from different materials. Likely every kind of naturally-forming block was represented here in zombie-town.

"I always wondered what endermen did with the blocks they stole," Crafter said at his side. "Likely they brought them to these zombie-towns."

Gameknight grunted and nodded his head.

The small houses lined the edges of the cavern and crept inward toward the center. A clear area sat right in the middle; it was the zombies' gathering area. At the center of the chamber was a platform made of obsidian. Gameknight couldn't tell how large it was, but he could still remember the zombie king, Xa-Tul, standing on something similar, right before he rescued Monet113.

Sparkling green HP fountains dotted the perimeter of the gathering area, the green embers splashing on the ground and disappearing. Gameknight remembered these fountains from other zombie-towns, but for some reason these one didn't look as if they were working correctly. Instead of a constant stream of emerald sparks cascading up into the air, these fountains were sputtering like a squirt gun with too little water. Gameknight was just about to say something about it to Crafter when a sorrowful moan echoed through the chamber.

"Keep that zombie quiet," Gameknight whispered to those behind him.

"It wasn't our zombie," Digger said. "It came from somewhere in the zombie-town."

Gameknight gazed across the chamber. He could see movement near the far wall. Zombies were coming out of a tunnel that descended into darkness. A handful of the monsters shuffled up the stairs, then moved to the nearest HP fountain. The monsters stood within the emerald shower and absorbed the green sparks, rejuvenating their

HP. After a few minutes, then moved back into the dark passage and disappeared from sight.

"Come on," the User-that-is-not-a-user said. "Leave some guards here with the zombie. Make sure it stays quiet, or else."

Digger nodded, then assigned some guards to watch over their prisoner. When he returned, the army moved down the stairs that led to the floor of the chamber. Running between the buildings, everyone was on edge, expecting monsters to jump out of every doorway or come charging around the next corner. But surprisingly, they wove their way through the disorganized community unseen.

Finally, the NPC army reached the far side of the cavern. Gameknight moved along the rough-hewn wall and approached the dark passage where he'd seen the zombie emerge. He could hear their growls and moans down in the shadows, but couldn't tell how many were there. Some of the warriors moved to the front of the tunnel, ready to charge down, but the User-that-is-not-a-user waved them back. He wasn't sure how many there were, and didn't want to take the chance of being vastly outnumbered. They had a sizable force with them, and could easily deal with any random monsters that might appear, but he still wanted to be careful about running into a large group of zombies.

"I'll go down and see how many there are," Gameknight whispered to a group of NPCs. "Everyone be ready and stay quiet."

Crafter nodded his head, then turned and whispered to Digger, who relayed the message down the line. Gameknight patted his friend on the shoulder, then headed down the stone stairway, diamond sword in hand. But after descending three steps, he felt a cold, wet nose nuzzle against his left hand. Looking down, he saw a wolf at his side. Glancing over his shoulder, he found Herder grinning a massive grin. Gameknight chuckled, then headed down the stairway with both of them.

He descended a dozen steps into darkness. The moans of the zombies grew louder as he went, their sorrowful moans filling the air with a sadness that highlighted the misery of their lives. These were unhappy creatures that wanted everyone else to share in their despair.

As he grew closer, Gameknight could start to identify individual monsters in the growling echoes; there was definitely more than one monster down there. Gripping his sword firmly, he followed the passage as it turned to the right, then plunged downward.

The end of the stairway was now visible. Apparently, the steps led into a large, well-lit room, though the color of the light was strange. It was a strange sort of mustard yellowish-brown illumination, as if it were the mixture of multiple flickering sources.

Gameknight moved to the end of the stairway and peered into the chamber. He saw three large obsidian rings, each filled with a different sparkling color: one purple, one green and the third a sickly yellow. Standing near the portal were fifteen zombies, each coated in gold armor and each holding a shining gold sword.

Before he could prevent it, the wolf next to him growled and let out a loud angry howl. All the zombies instantly turned toward the sound and glared

into the shadows, their dark eyes filled with hate.
Then they charged straight at Gameknight999.

COMING SOON:
SYSTEM OVERLOAD: HEROBRINE'S
REVENGE BOOK THREE